# taking the shot

## S.L. FORRESTER

Copyright © 2023 S.L.Forrester

All rights reserved. This book or any portion thereof may not be reproduced or used in any manner whatsoever without the express written permission of the publisher except for the use of brief quotations in a book review.

Independently published.

This is a work of fiction. Names, characters, places, and incidents either are the product of the author's imagination or are used factiously. Any resemblance to actual persons, living or dead, events or locals is entirely coincidental.

Cover designer: CPR Designs

Editor: Katie Rehberg

# Contents

1. Ash — 1
2. Jace — 19
3. Ash — 37
4. Jace — 47
5. Ash — 63
6. Jace — 73
7. Ash — 87
8. Jace — 112
9. Ash — 126
10. Jace — 142
11. Ash — 159
12. Jace — 164
13. Ash — 172
14. Jace — 175
15. Ash — 186
16. Jace — 202

| 17. Ash | 218 |
| 18. Jace | 239 |
| 19. Ash | 259 |
| Epilogue-Ash | 272 |
| Acknowledgments | 274 |
| About Author | 276 |

# Chapter 1
## Ash

Fucking kid! How hard is it to put his dirty clothes IN the basket instead of on the floor beside it? I told him to have his room straight before his dad picked him up, now look who gets to do it on a Friday night. It's fine. Everything is fine. I will clean up this mess and sit on the couch with my Jack and Coke while watching my favorite show, *FRIENDS*. You know what, no! I am sexy and single, I should go out. Well, maybe not sexy, but definitely passing. Somewhat. I lack nice boobs, a flat stomach, and flawless skin. My choice of clothing is more for my comfort than for the male's attention. Oversized t-shirt and jeans for when I leave my house and pjs while at home. I don't think I even own anything nice to wear. Silas's dad never cared what I wore. Or at least that's what he said.

I believed him until I found polaroids of a human version of Jessica Rabbit between the mattress and box spring. I mean I get it, but still. Fuck that guy, he can eat a dick. I am going to put on makeup and actually brush my hair. My only problem now is that I have no idea where a bar is. That's okay, nothing a little internet search won't fix. It takes a whole five seconds to find a decently rated drinking spot and it is right around the corner. Now there is no excuse, I'm going! I put on my AC/DC shirt and jeans with the holes in the knees. For this special occasion, I am pulling out my black Sk8-Hi Vans with a bright white stripe across the side.

As I stand in front of my bathroom mirror, I talk myself up.

*"Okay Ash, you can do this. What's the worst that could happen?"*

I go there and have a drink alone and then go home. Or I could have more than one drink and find some random to bring home. No, don't bring him home. Just screw him in the bathroom. Or her, honestly, I'm not picky at this point. As long as I don't have to hold a vibrator, I'll be happy. I want to feel an actual tongue on me. I don't even remember what that's like. Whatever, stop trying to put this off and get the fuck out of the house. Okay okay okay. Keys, phone, wallet, pepper spray, condom, gum. Throw it all in my tiny purse and I am ready to go. That should be all I need. I would call a friend to tell them where I'll be but I chose to have none. I haven't found a person out there that could deal with me and my anxiety.

Why am I still not out the door?

Stop thinking about it and just go!

Walking out the door, I pull GPS up on my phone. Finding the bar and clicking the directions button, I get in my gray SUV and start driving. When I get there the parking lot looks pretty dead. Is this the right place? Well, I'm here now, might as well go in and see what it's about. When I pull the door to the place open, I find that it is actually packed. But where are their cars? Maybe they Ubered, that's smart if they plan to get shitfaced. Damn, I drove and I don't want to leave my car here overnight. I guess I can't drink as much as I wanted. Fuck. I make my way to the gold at the end of the rainbow, the alcohol. The bartender is pretty hot, they always are.

"Hey sweetheart, what can I get you?" he asks.

"Can I please have a Jack and Coke?" I give him my sweetest smile.

"Coming right up." He doesn't do the fancy moves that I've seen on tv, but I get the drink all the same. After I pay him the stupid amount of money for it, I turn around to see the crowd and immediately turn back around toward the guy.

"Everything okay?" He has this concerned look on his face.

"Yes, I usually try to avoid crowds." I know I sound so stupid right now because why come to a fucking bar on a Friday night if I can't be around a lot of people.

"You can always stick around here and keep me entertained." He winks and gives a little smirk. I look him up and down to get the full picture of this gorgeous man. He is in dark brown steel-toe boots, dark blue jeans and a white t-shirt with the sleeves slightly rolled up. He has tattoos peeking out on both arms and what looks like a rose on the side of his neck. His tan skin and chocolate eyes make me want to eat him up. Just as I am about to introduce myself, some asshat interrupts.

"He's not into you," he points out.

"Excuse me?" What the fuck is this guy's problem?

"He's. Not. Into. You," he says slower.

"You just walked up. How could you possibly know? We could be sleeping together." Shit, I wish I was getting down and dirty with him.

"Are you fucking him?" he asks, looking very cocky.

"No, but you can't just walk up and start assuming things," I say as a matter of factly.

"He flirts with everybody. The more he convinces you that he wants to get you naked, the more you tip him," this guy thinks he knows everything.

I look back at the bartender and he just smiles and walks away. Seriously? "Now that you've run off my eye candy for the night, what do you want?" I put my hand on my hip.

"Maybe I was just trying to help you out," he says but I see the little twinkle in his eyes.

"Did it look like I needed or even wanted help?" I just wanted to have the bartender's head between my thighs.

"If some guy saw you desperately flirting with the bartender then they would think that you're an easy lay," he says like he's not thinking about doing the same damn thing. This fucker.

"Who said that I didn't want to fall into bed with a stranger?" His baby blue eyes darken and he slowly takes two steps closer. As he places his hand on the bar counter,

I can't help but notice the veins going up his arm. And oh God, those muscles. My body is fully aware of the sexy, around six-foot tall man with messy dark brown hair mere inches from it. I feel the wetness between my thighs and I slightly push them together in hopes that he doesn't notice. The way he's looking at me tells me that he can see that I'm about to explode. Thinking about making those couple of inches between us disappear...

"Well, I'll leave you to it then. I hope it works out." He has a big ass smile on his face, turns, and walks away.

Are you fucking kidding me? What the hell?

I need to get myself together. I look around to see if anybody just witnessed that fun little scene, luckily nobody seemed to care. I get my purse and head toward the restroom, maybe it will be empty and I can rub one out. I walk around the couple that are making out in front of the damn door. Like, get the fuck out of the way, go to an alley like normal people. Pulling the door open, I feel a body pushing me into the room.

"Jeeze, if you just wait then I'll get out of your way," I tell whatever dipshit it is.

"I think you want to be in my way." That voice. That deep, rough voice. It's the asshat that got me worked up and then walked away.

"Who the hell do you think you are, pushing me around and then assuming I want you," I ask him in the snarkiest tone that I can muster up. He grabs my arm and pulls me into a small ass stall.

"Are you into watching me pee because it isn't really my thing?" I let my sarcasm come out to play.

"Say no at any point and I'll stop," he says with his teeth clenched together. That takes me by surprise and I think I should be scared but it only turns me on. A man taking consent seriously... sign me the fuck up.

He turns us so that now my back is to the door, takes both of my wrists, and moves them over my head. He takes a step closer and I'm being pressed onto the door. We stare at each other for only a second and he dips his head to my neck. I get lost in him while he licks, bites, and kisses my favorite place. I push my hips into him to show how much I like it and then his hands fall from my wrists and go to pull the hem of my shirt up. I hesitate and his mouth is off of me immediately and he takes a step back. I grab his shirt and pull him back to me.

"My boobs are disappointingly small." He bends down enough to where his face is lined up with my chest and I hold my breath as he pushes my shirt and bra up. He looks at my pierced nipples and smiles. Then his mouth is on me, sucking and nipping while his hand is squeezing my other boob. And the tingling between my thighs is back. He stands back up and whispers in my ear,

"Anything more than a mouthful is a waste," I swear I almost came just from those words. He bites my lip and then starts kissing me. It's sloppy and needy. I have never had somebody kiss me like this before. Like he wants to devour me, like he has to have me or he will be in pain. I push my hands up his shirt and Oh My God! Abs for days. I rake my nails down him from his chest to the happy trail that leads to what I'm hoping will leave me happy. That makes him lose it. He starts unbuttoning my pants, pushing them down just below my ass.

"Are you wet?" His voice is husky.

"Too scared to find out for yourself?" The smirk that he gives me makes my pussy cry out.

"Remember, just say no," he reminds me.

"You seem highly confident." After I say that, he doesn't hold back. His two fingers put a little pressure at my entrance.

"Hold on tight," he orders.

"Are you talking to me or my pussy?"

"Both." Then he shoves both fingers into me. They are thick and have me biting my lip until I taste metallic. I thought he was going to keep going until I cum but he quickly took his fingers out and wiped my juices on his pants.

"Well, aren't you the sweetest?" I roll my eyes.

"I don't play with meaningless women that I have a quick fuck with." I was right, he is an asshat but my body is stubborn and still wants him.

"Get a condom," I tell him before we go any further.

"I don't have one but it's okay because I'm clean." He has got to be kidding me. I push him off and I know my expression is having a whole-ass conversation.

"I don't give a fuck if your dick has never seen a hole before. I have one and you are going to wear it if you want this 'meaningless fuck'." I grab the condom out of my purse and tear the wrapper open.

"Are you going to stand there looking stupid or are you going to take your dick out?" He quickly unbuckles his belt, pops open his pants, and pushes them down. "Who wears jeans with snap-on buttons anymore?" I ask but he doesn't say another word and rolls the condom on. I push my pants down the rest of the way and step out of them. My shoes come off with them but I quickly slide them back on. I can't stand feet. His hand slides down my thigh and once he gets to the back of my knee, he jerks up so that one leg is draped over his arm. Thankfully I'm flexible or this would be a bitch. With his other hand, he lines himself up and thrusts into me. All of the way. He's so thick and it stings a little but I like it. He doesn't take it slow and he's definitely not gentle, but I didn't say no so he keeps going. I have to hold onto his shoulders so that I don't fall on my face, or end up in the toilet. His other hand grabs my waist and squeezes. He slams into me so hard that I can't help but let out a moan and my head falls back to the door. Forgetting my surroundings, I start getting loud.

"You better keep that pretty mouth shut if you don't want everybody to hear." With that being said, I come back to reality and notice that I hear multiple girls talking. Damn, they definitely heard me. How could they not? Maybe this is a normal thing and nobody cares. I almost go down the rabbit hole with my thoughts but then he moves his hand from my waist and grabs my jaw. Not forcefully but not gently either. "I am right here, not out there." And then he pulls out and slams back into me. I wrap my arms around his neck and pull him closer so that I can bite down on his neck. That seems to turn him on even more because his rhythm gets faster and a bit unhinged.

"Cum," is all he says. I hope he doesn't expect me to do that on command. When I don't do as he says, he looks at me like he's been denied. I go to fake it but he whispers in my ear, "If you don't give me what I want, I'll open this door and let everybody watch." I stare at him to see if he's serious. He starts to move to open the door and I couldn't stop myself, the dominance alone makes my eyes close so hard that I see stars. I clench around him and he takes my mouth with his and pushes his tongue in. My hand roams up to grab onto his hair and I try so hard not to scream when the fire in my core starts. A couple more thrusts and I'm flying. I hear him growl into my mouth and I almost cum again.

When he stops moving, he lets my leg drop and we just stand there trying to catch our breath. After what seems like a short minute, he pulls the condom off and ties it. I start to put my pants back on while he throws it in the trash and gets himself together. He looks at me and smiles. "Thanks, catcha' later." And walks out of the stall, leaving me there without another word.

Just wow.

I know that I basically begged for it but he could have at least told me his name or literally anything else. I finish pulling my pants up in a rush and walk out of the stall to a group of girls passing around a joint. Ignoring them and heading to the sink to wash my hands, because I'm a lady, my phone rings. I quickly dry my hands off and take my phone out. It's Silas.

"Hey baby, how are you?" I try to put a little bit of happiness in my voice.

"I got a call from Coach Jace earlier today and he told me that I made the team." He makes it sound like it's no big deal but I know he is bouncing off the wall with excitement.

"That's great news! When do you start?" I ask him, hoping it falls on my time instead of his dad's.

"Monday, after school. Don't worry about the gear, dad said he's got it." Of-fucking-course he does. I should be happy that he's helping with it but I'm still feeling a bit salty toward him.

"Okay, well I'm very excited for you! See, you were so worried after tryouts and I told you that you're amazing on the field. It's like you were born to play soccer." I had to talk him out of leaving the field the entire time.

"Yeah, yeah, Mom. I just called to tell you to buy more gatorade for the fridge. I gotta go. Bye." He rushes off.

"I love you." I never hang up without telling him that he's loved.

"I love you too, Mom." He spits out and then hangs up. Nothing like having a child in sports. I mean that in the worst way. As the parent, I have to bring snacks and drinks during my week, take him to practice three times a week, and a game once a week. His room always smells like something died in there, but the one thing that is the hardest - playing nice with the other moms. I would rather poke my fucking eyes out. But my son loves the game so I have to suck it up and smile. I put my phone back in my purse and walk out of the bathroom. I got what I came here for so now I get to go back to my warm house and pjs. I see Mr. Asshat before I get to the exit door of the bar, and all I can do is smile and flip him off. He smirks and goes back to talking to his group.

The weekend was like every other. I had my first iced coffee, started laundry, washed dishes and laid on the couch watching t.v.. It's Sunday evening and I'm waiting for Silas to get home from his dads. The irritation from Friday night hasn't gone away. Who says 'catcha' later' after a hookup? What an asshole. But moving on. I'm almost done making spaghetti when I hear the door open.

"Mom?" I speed walk to the living room to see my son drop his school bag, weekend bag, and new bigger duffle bag on the floor.

"Hey sweetheart, I missed you. How was your weekend?" I ask even though I know he had a great time.

"Good. We went to some stores to get all of my soccer stuff," he says as he takes his new bag to the couch and starts taking everything out to show me. "Dad got me all the stuff that my friends have." His face lights up as he takes out his size 5 soccer ball, shin guards, knee-high socks, lace bands, cleats and gym shorts.

"Wow, he got you set up. But do you know what he forgot?" He looks around at everything, thinking.

"What?" He asks, very confused.

"A year's supply of deodorant. You stink! Take everything to your room and then get a shower. Dinner is almost done." I play around with him but he really does smell like he didn't bathe at all while he was gone.

"I don't stink, I smell like a man." I try my best not to burst out laughing.

"A man? Is that what men smell like? Maybe that's why I'm single. I don't think I could be around this smell all the time." He starts laughing with me then gets off the couch, grabs his things, and heads to his room. Great, now my couch stinks. Nothing a little Fabric Febreze won't fix. I also light my favorite candle, watermelon lemonade, just to be safe. After a minute of taking in the fruity smell, I have a small heart attack and run to the stove to check on the food. Calming my breathing when I see that everything is okay, I turn the stove off. I make Silas and myself a bowl and then go to his room to tell him that it's time to eat. As I get closer to his room, I hear a faint moaning sound. It sounds like girls though. Oh My God! He's watching porn. Nope, I'm not dealing with this today. Turning around to head back to the kitchen, I call his dad.

**"Hello."**

"Did you know your son watches porn?"

**"Yeah, I told him what websites to look up on his phone."**

"What the fuck is wrong with you?"

**"It's normal for kids his age. Are you telling me that you never touched yourself when you were 15?"**

"Of course I did, I was fucking you so I needed something to get me off. But I didn't have my parents show me where to go!"

**"Don't make it sound like that. I didn't look the website up and show him. He came to me with questions and as his dad, I talked to him about it. Look, he can either go out and have sex, which could be dangerous if he isn't told about protection, or he can watch it on his phone in the privacy of his room. By himself."** I guess he's not a complete dipshit after all.

"Okay, fine. I didn't think about it like that. It just caught me off guard. Yuck, I could have gone the rest of my life without knowing about this."

**"Yeah well, he's growing up. It happens."**

"Thanks. That helps me out so much."

**"You know, your sarcasm does get old."**

"I'm sure fake boobs in your face make you forget all about it."

"Really? Can you move on from that? It's been eight months. You must not be getting laid."

"I got pregnant at 15. You were there, remember? Apparently, the porn that I was watching wasn't good enough. I thought you loved me. I guess being together for the past 16 years was just for the hell of it."

"We were kids. I didn't know what else to do."

"That counts for the first few years. What about when you actually grew up? You're a fucking adult! You can't use that excuse."

"You know what, I don't have time for this. I will talk to you the Friday after next when I pick Silas up."

Click. He just hung up on me. He fucked up and was called out on it and HE hung up on ME. Maybe I was wrong for even bringing it up. Ugh, my head hurts now. I need a drink. Heading to the fridge, my mind starts wandering off to Friday night. Why am I still thinking about this? Oh right, because I have never had sex like that before. And the way he fit inside of me, mmm. I start to feel myself getting wet just thinking about it. I have to stop, this is crazy. I am never going to see that man again. We didn't exchange names, numbers, or anything. Silas walks into the kitchen, bringing me back to earth. "How was your shower?" I ask him.

"It was like any other shower." He sounds bored with this conversation.

"Do you want to tell me anything?" I don't want to call him out but it's something that needs to be addressed.

"Nope. Can I eat now?" He tries to change the subject.

"Go ahead. Your bowl is on the table. What do you want to drink?" I'll move on for now.

"Sweet tea, please." Well, at least he still has his manners. I'm not going to bring the other thing up until he wants to talk about it. I pour a glass of red wine for me and a cup of tea for him.

"Are you excited to meet your team tomorrow?" I try to get him back in a good mood.

"Yeah, I guess," he answers nonchalantly.

"Calm down, your excitement is showing." He rolls his eyes but smiles. The rest of the meal is in silence. I honestly don't like listening to him eat spaghetti because he likes to slurp the noodles up. I'm almost positive he does it just to annoy me, so I don't let him see my irritation. After I clean up from dinner, I go and enjoy a hot shower. The water is hot enough that the devil himself would back away. If my skin isn't bright red when I get out, then it wasn't good. Stepping out of the shower, I stand there with my eyes closed just to breathe in the steamy room. It's the small things that I enjoy now that Silas isn't a small kid anymore. I used to take a shower with him banging on the door because he needed something. No, it could never wait until I finished. After I'm dressed in my pajama shorts and a t-shirt, I head back to the bathroom to braid my hair and brush my teeth. So happy that it is bedtime. My favorite time of day.

Monday morning was crazy busy at the coffee shop. Of course it is because who the hell likes Mondays? Well, there is the cat lady that comes in every morning. She has been trying to get me to make this place one of those 'coffee and cat' places. The ones that have cats just walking around jumping in people's laps. That's a hard pass. She told me her name once but I completely forgot it and I don't want to be rude and ask her again. So I just smile and nod. My alarm starts going off on my phone for me to pick Silas up and take him to his soccer practice. I turn it off and call him to make sure he has everything and is ready to go when I get home. I'm lucky enough that my son makes friends a little easier than I do. His best friend, Cody, has one of those nice moms and she takes him home after school.

"Hey," he answers.

"Hey, I'm getting in the car now, are you ready to go?" I ask him.

"Yes, Mom," he responds.

"Do you have your shin guards?" I start going down my mental checklist.

"Yes, Mom," he starts to sound annoyed.

"What about socks? Are you wearing the right socks?" I have to ask him because sometimes he isn't the brightest.

"Yes, Mom. I am wearing everything that I'm supposed to. I don't want to get there and look stupid." He shuts down that conversation.

"Okay, I'll be there in ten minutes. Be ready to walk out of the door when I pull up," I tell him.

"I'll just go wait outside," he says, annoyed.

"Even better. I love you," I say quickly before he hangs up.

"I love you too," he mumbles and the line goes dead.

I pull into my driveway and he is standing there, just as he said. Sometimes he surprises me. When I put the SUV in park, he throws his bag in the back and then joins me in the front.

"How was your day at school?" I start us off.

"It was pretty boring. But that girl that I like smiled at me. That was cool," he says with the biggest smile.

"Are you planning to talk to her in this lifetime?" He has been talking about her for months now.

"These things take time, Mom. It's been forever since you had to go to school. You can't just walk up to a girl and start talking to her." He explains to me like I'm stupid.

"I'm not that old. I know you are nervous but someone has to walk up and say hey." Our conversation got cut short when we pull up to the field.

"Please don't embarrass me," he begs.

"I promise I won't talk to anybody. But I do want to meet your coach." He jumps out of the car before I can put it in park. "Well okay then." I get out of the car and walk toward this tall guy with a black hat, dark blue shirt, black gym shorts, and cleats. I assume that's the coach. When I get to him, he's facing the opposite way.

"Excuse me, but are you the coach?" He turns around to look at me. "What the..."

## Chapter 2

## Jace

..."Fuck," she says. It's her. The smartass from the bar. I haven't stopped thinking about her since I walked out of that bathroom stall. I hated the way I left but she seemed like the type that only wanted to get off and move on. I was just helping her out so we didn't have to do that awkward stare and silence, waiting for the other to say something. But the way she is looking at me right now, I think I messed up.

"Please tell me you aren't the coach," she asks, hopeful.

"I'm not the coach," I say just for shits and giggles.

"Thank God." She lets out a breath, relieved.

"Oh I actually am, I was just telling you what you wanted to hear." If looks could kill, I would have just died. But she's so cute, mad like this. "I think I can actually see smoke coming out of your ears. Don't you get tired of being mad all the time?"

"You don't even know me." She rolls her eyes.

"No, but I do know what you feel like wrapped around my cock." And I haven't stopped thinking about it but there's no way in hell I'll admit that to her. Not that she would give a shit anyways. Heat rises from her neck to her cheeks, she remembers too. I wonder if she lays in bed thinking about it late at night.

"There are kids everywhere! You can't walk around saying those things. Actually, I would prefer it if you didn't talk about it at all." Oh that is never going to happen.

"What if I just think about it? Maybe give you a wink when I do? Of course, I would basically be blinking at that point." That makes her glow even redder. It's going to be ridiculously fun toying with her. She gets worked up so easily. "Which one is yours?"

"What?" She asks, looking confused.

"Kid, which kid is yours?" I exclaimed.

"Oh, umm, Silas Miller. The short one with the shaggy brown hair." Ah, the kid that needs more help than what practice can give him. His old coach said that he was good but a bit slower at making it click in his head. "Look, can we just not do this? Silas is nervous but he really wants to be on your team. I don't know what's so special about you but he was really excited when he got the phone call. We are going to pretend it didn't happen and move on," she says and starts to walk away but I can't let that happen.

"Okay but don't come back to me when you see me running on the field, I know how you girls love that." I try to get her even more pissy.

"Good thing I'm not a girl. I'm a grown-ass woman." And with that, she walks to the sideline and sits on the grass. I heard bits and pieces about Silas's dad but I can't pursue her until I get the whole story. I know it's a little late for the touching without knowing but I didn't know who she was then. I'm not a cheating piece of shit like my ex. I may not be in a relationship but fucking her knowing she's in one, it's the same thing. God, I hope she's not with him anymore because I can't stop thinking about her. But right now, my head needs to be in this sport. Start strong, finish strong.

"Alright guys, come take a knee. Hurry up, y'all can go back to your mommies when we're done." Oh jeez, this is going to be a long season if they plan to be this slow. "So, my name is Coach Jace. Just in case y'all don't know it for whatever reason. Our team name is the *Gladiators* and we are going to do it justice. Look around, this is your family. You will fight with each other, laugh with each other and yes, even cry with each other. We will have each other's backs on and off the field. I know they say to go out there on game day and have fun, and we will but we are also going to take it seriously. When you put your jerseys on, nothing else matters but this team. Everything at home, your girlfriend dumping you, your sibling punching you in the face. All of that magically erases from your thoughts. This could even be an outlet for you. All in all, let's have a great season. Now get up and give me three laps." That went well. I can't help but look for the little smartass, I really need to ask for her name. Just as I'm about to walk to her, a mom walks up.

"Hey, so I was just wondering if you could come over to my house one day to help my baby? Some one-on-one.

His dad is never home to help him and he just needs a man to play with." Shit. She's doing this hair thing around her finger. Pushing her fake breasts up, and getting a little too close.

"I can run some plays with him on this field anytime. As long as you don't mind dropping him off and leaving. Kids play better when their parents aren't around." It's hard not to start laughing when her face falls. Just another desperate mom needing attention. Not my type, also that big ass ring on her finger is a huge stop sign. Anyways, back to what I was doing. Looking back at her, I can't help but smile. She's sitting on the grass with her legs stretched out and her ankles crossed. The great thing about springtime, shorts. She's got on jean shorts and a light blue t-shirt with her hair up in a ponytail. She has her eyes closed, taking in the sun. I want to say something but I'm enjoying standing over her watching. That sounds creepy.

"You know, your girlfriend might not want you over here." She saw that. Wait, why would she care?

"Do I hear a bit of jealousy?" I try to flirt but I've been out of the game for too long.

"I don't think so. I'm just not the type to talk to somebody's boyfriend." She's interested. It's all uphill from here.

"Good thing that's just another mom. I don't have a girlfriend. If I did, I wouldn't have been inside you Friday night. This brings me to the reason why I came over here.

Are you still with Silas's dad?" I have to know before I go any further.

"I'm no cheater. I don't believe in that kinda thing," she says.

"That doesn't answer my question." I'm not going to let her talk around this one.

"No, I am not with him, or anybody for that matter. Now that you have that off of your chest, go do your job." Perfect. I'm not even trying to hide my happiness.

"I'm a volunteer. I actually like helping the kids out." Though a paycheck would be a plus.

"You're just perfect." That mouth of hers, the things I want to do with it.

"Well I mean, of course, I am." I give her a wink as I start to turn around. Damnit! I forgot to ask her name. The boys are almost done with their last lap, I guess it'll have to wait. But I did get the green light on getting to know her more. These boys are actually in good shape. Nobody fell to the ground when they finished. "Alright guys, go get some water, and then we will start with some suicides." I can't help but smile when they all start booing. That one is always the most hated. I line up cones and stand back and then take a quick glance to see if my little smartass is looking. To my excitement, she is. Of course, she is. "Alright, y'all are going to do it ten times. Line up!" They are way too slow. "Hustle!" There we go, that got them going for now. "Ready? On my whistle." I put my brand new, shiny silver whistle on my lips and blow.

They all immediately jump up and start to run but I can tell they're starting to get tired. I can't help but keep coming back to Silas. He doesn't seem like he needs extra help, maybe he has problems with the ball. I guess it's time to find out. Walking to my soccer bag and the net of balls that I brought, I feel eyes on me. I look up to see a man standing next to my girl. Okay, she's not mine yet. I get the vest for the goalie and a ball then walk back to the team. "Alright, guys, water break, and then we're going to do some free kicks. After that, y'all can go." I'm starting to get irritated with the man still standing by her. She hasn't gotten up and she's deep in conversation with him. Did she lie about not seeing anybody? "Hey, Silas, come here for a minute," I yell out.

"What's up, Coach?" He jogs over.

"Who is that man over there with your mom?" I try not to sound too jealous.

"Oh, that's my dad," he says with something in his voice that I can't quite put my finger on.

"Oh, okay. I thought... Nevermind. Thanks." I just shake my head. He's here, with her.

"He doesn't live with us. He and my mom broke up a few months ago. He usually doesn't come to practice, but he does make it to all of my games. Why did you want to know?" He sounds intrigued.

"No reason, just curious." I try to make it seem like it's nothing.

"Look, if you're after my mom, good luck." He gives a small laugh and shakes his head.

"Why do you say that?" Now I'm confused.

"She hasn't dated anyone since my dad cheated on her. They tried to keep why they split from me but I put it together when my dad moved in with another girl. So like I said, good luck." He doesn't hold back from the details.

"Man, go drink your water." He turns and runs over to his mom. I hope he doesn't tell her about what was just said. I want to talk to her but I think I'll save that conversation for when her ex isn't standing right beside her. I mean, I don't care but she might. Getting my head back to where it's supposed to be, I call them to the field. "Alright, let's find our goalie."

My dick being this hard is making driving a little difficult. I can't let it keep pushing against my zipper, it's starting to hurt. Unzipping my pants, I pull my favorite part out. That feels better. But the brain in my head isn't the one thinking when I start to slowly stroke myself. I have to cum, it can't wait until I get home. I pull off on the side of the road and start taking care of my problem. I take a look out my windows to make sure nobody is walking up to see what's going on. But then I start thinking about her and my eyes close. What if she pulled up right now and caught me? My imagination starts and my eyes close.

*She knocks on my window and I roll it down.*

*"What are you doing in there?" Looking down at what's in front of her. "Oh wow, okay." She opens my door. "Let me help you out." She's wearing a flowy sundress and when she sits in my lap, my hands run up her thighs. Making my way under the hem, I notice she's not wearing any panties. My dick is standing at attention between us. She grabs it with one hand and my shoulder with the other. I feel her wet folds sliding up and down one side of my shaft.*

I spit in my hand and start to squeeze harder and move my hand up and down faster.

*"I may not know much about soccer, Coach, but I would love to play with your balls." Holy fuck, please. She takes her hand off my shoulder and cradles them. Oh, God. She moves her fingers to push them around and then stops. I go to ask why she stopped but then I see her get up to position her pussy over my dick. We hold each other's stare as she slowly sits and takes me. Little by little. Her plump pink lips part and she lets out a quiet moan as she is fully seated. I go to lift her but she grabs my hands and slaps her ass with them. "You hold on while I ride you." Then she starts moving up and down. Her hand sits on my chest and slowly travels up to my neck. She doesn't squeeze hard but puts a little pressure. She starts moaning loudly. "Pour yourself in me."*

I pick up the shirt in the passenger seat and put it over the head of my dick and shoot my seed in it. With my eyes closed and my head leaning back on the headrest, I take a few breaths to calm my heart rate. Open my eyes and look around to make sure nobody decided to watch the show. Luckily I'm still by myself. I clean up and tuck it back into where it belongs. Checking the road for incoming traffic, I pull out and drive home. It's only a 5-minute drive from where I stopped. Once I pull up to my three-bedroom two bath home, I grab my dirty shirt and head inside.

I bought this house so that I could start a family with my ex but that went to hell when I found pictures of her sucking somebody's dick on her phone. She left it unlocked and I went to take a picture of the ring I bought her, just a little surprise, and that's when I saw it. Perfect timing really, saved me from proposing and ruining my life. That was two years ago and I haven't tried to settle down again. The ring was returned right after I confronted her. I wasn't wasting any more time with that one.

Putting those thoughts out of my mind, I head to the washing machine and throw the shirt in. I may be a man but I'm not messy. I can't stand for anything to be out of place. Smelling under my arm, I cringe and go take a shower. My shower was made for two, I love the space. Turning it on to a little hotter than lukewarm, I strip down and get in. I stand under the shower head and feel the water hit my head and run down my hair, over my eyes, and my lips. It drips to my chest and down my body.

Today has been a long day but at least my team isn't bad. Sure, they could use some work but they are still just kids. I pour soap on my loofa and start to wash my body.

My mind has its own plans when I get down to the V just below my abs. She pops up in my head again and I look down. "You have got to be kidding me." My body is acting like a teenager again. I try to steer my mind to literally anything else but it's a fail. I might as well take care of this, again. I lean back onto the shower wall and let my imagination run wild.

*She's on her knees looking up at me with her big hazel eyes.*

*"I want you in my mouth." I nod my head and she licks from the base to the head. Her tongue circles the tip and then she wraps her lips around me and takes all of it. She doesn't stop. She has one hand on my thigh and the other playing with my balls. Her eyes are watering and she starts gagging but she doesn't slow down. I warn her, "I'm going to cum in your mouth if you don't stop."*

*She pops my dick out of her mouth, smiles, and says, "Make sure you pull my hair when you do."*

That's all it takes and I'm cumming down the drain. I have got to get my shit together. I finish cleaning myself, get out and dry off. Putting on gray sweatpants and head to the kitchen to make myself some dinner.

Stepping outside and feeling how nice the February weather is, I decide to walk to work. This time of year is usually still pretty chilly in the mornings but this year it's perfect. I pass by a few runners and smile. I'm one of those rare morning people that everybody hates. Not that I can help it, I've tried to stay up late at night and sleep in, it never works out and I end up hating myself for it. The one bad thing about morning time is that everybody is getting coffee. I have passed by this little coffee shop every day and never had time to stop in.

Looking at my watch, I notice that I'm actually early for once. I guess I finally get to see what this place is about. My buddies tell me their wives love it, but I do hear the complaint that they never serve pumpkin spice. Doesn't matter to me, I like my coffee black. Apparently, it's a big thing for the female community. I walk into the shop and take it all in. Straight ahead is the counter to order with the menu written on a huge chalkboard on the wall behind their heads. To the left is one long rectangular table and a few small round tables. The right side is just like the left. It looks like I got here at the perfect time because the crowd seems to be leaving with their drinks.

"Hi, welcome to Ash's coffee house, what can I get for you?" A small blonde behind the counter asks.

"Just a black coffee please," I tell her with my sweetest voice.

"Would you like any cream or sugar?" She asks sweetly.

"Nope, just black." I try not to let any negative tone come out.

"Yes sir, that will be three dollars and twenty-eight cents." She gives me the total.

"That's crazy for a plain coffee." I go to pull out my wallet to pay when I hear a voice coming from the door behind the menu wall. That voice, I know that voice. It's the one that keeps me up at night. She walks out and stops when she sees me. "Well, hello. I didn't know you worked here."

The girl taking my money starts to laugh and says, "She kinda owns the place."

Ignoring my question, she starts talking to the girl behind the counter.

"Clara, give him his money back. This one is on the house." She makes eye contact with me. "If my coffee is too expensive for you, I can recommend some great coffee makers for your kitchen." The things that I want to do to that smart mouth. I just smirk because now I have her name. Clara gives me my coffee and I wave off the money. I tell her thank you, then turn to leave.

"I'll see you at practice, Ash." With that, I walk out the door. I can't help but have a stupid smile on my face for the rest of my walk.

Once I get to work, I try to stop smiling but that failed time as my friend looks at me. I hurry to the locker room but she isn't having that.

"Excuse me but your face looks funny. Is that a smile?" My best friend asks.

"Izzy, I smile all the time." Rolling my eyes at her.

"Yes, but this one is different. Did you get laid?" She likes knowing all of the details.

"Remember that girl from Friday night?" Of course, I had to tell her about that.

"The girl that you hooked up with? How did you describe her again? Oh yeah, a smart mouth and a body that you can lick for days." We both start laughing. "So, what about her?"

"She owns that coffee shop right down the road that's always busy," I inform her.

"Ash's Coffee House? I love that place. It has the best caramel frappe." She makes a noise of approval.

"I will never understand how you can drink that junk. It's not even coffee at that point," I tell her this every time I see one in her hand.

"Whatever, just try not to stalk her. Ms. Beth is already waiting for you." Ms. Beth is the 68-year-old lady that I train. She came to me two years ago just wanting to build up some muscle to be able to open her jam jars. Now she says she just likes coming. I fill my water bottle up and walk over to the free weights.

"Good morning, Ms. Beth. How are you feeling?" I ask her with a friendly smile.

"Good morning, handsome. I feel great! But look at you, you look like you finally made it to the toy in your cereal box." She always has some off-the-wall saying.

"Ms. Beth, they don't put toys in them anymore. Did you eat your breakfast this morning? You know we can't do anything on an empty stomach." I have to remind her or she will never eat.

"Yes, I ate my bagel and a banana. Now don't change the subject. Give this old lady something to smile about." She enjoys grilling me.

"Fine, but we are going to train while I tell you. Let's start with ten reps of seated bicep curls. Each arm." I get the 10-pound weights and take them to her. She sits on the bench and stares at me.

"Oh mister, I am not starting until those lips start moving." I smile and start telling her the story.

"I met a girl. She is, mmm, different. She has something to say for everything. It's very infuriating when I try to talk to her and she starts smarting off at me." Ms. Beth finishes with one arm and starts laughing. "Next arm."

"Has she told you to leave her alone?" She asks.

"No, but she doesn't seem to enjoy my presence either." I shrug my shoulders and go with it.

"Maybe she just has her walls up and is scared to take a chance." Ms. Beth always has the knowledge to share.

"Her son is on my soccer team. He told me his dad cheated on her and they're over. I don't know if I should move on or try harder." I'm hoping that she will just give me the answer.

"You know the saying, if it's easy then it's not worth it? I think if you have an actual attraction then you should…what do the kids say…shoot your shot." I burst out laughing.

"I can't believe you just said that." She finishes her last curl and puts the weight on the floor beside her bench.

"You should take advantage of her son being there. Maybe offer some extra practice with him. Get him to like you and then sneak your way to his mom. If the kid doesn't like you, the mom won't either. But if you get him on your side, maybe he'll start talking his mom into spending time with you." She has a wicked spark in her eyes.

"Are you really suggesting I use this kid?" I make a show of looking appalled with my hand over my heart and my mouth open to make an o shape.

"Of course I am. Take the opportunity. Use the hell out of him." I stand there watching her and start to really think about this. He does have some problems with his kick. I guess I could help him out and in return, it helps me.

"Drink your water and then we can head to the chest press." I shake my head.

I haven't been to the coffee shop since Monday morning and now it's Wednesday afternoon and I'm headed to the field for practice. Today is going to be the day. I'm going to grow some balls and ask her out. I don't even remember the last time I asked somebody out. I did mess around with some women but I wouldn't call asking them to come back to my place as a date. Pulling into a spot, I look at the field and there are two people playing around. I get out of my BMW and walk around to the trunk to get my duffle and bag of extra soccer balls. I haul them to the goal and drop them.

Looking back up to the field, I see her. Ash and Silas running around kicking the ball. She's in some tight, black gym shorts and a white tight tank top. She's got her hair up in a ponytail and I can't help but watch the sweat run down her neck to her breast. Wearing a white shirt while running around is not the smartest thing, but I'm enjoying every bit of it. The sweat is making wet spots and I can almost see through it. I feel my dick getting hard. Stop, stop, stop. I close my eyes and let my head hang, we can't be doing this when there are kids around. Get it together. I wait until it goes back down and then open my eyes. They are headed towards me.

"Hey Silas, getting some practice in?" I call out.

"We don't have much room to play in our yard so I have to come out here," he says, a little out of breath.

"Well, you know we can schedule a time to meet up here if your mom can bring you? Any time you want." I try to encourage it but Ash jumps in on that one.

"Don't tell him that because he'll try to get you any chance he can. I'm sure you have a job and stuff to do." She tries to move past me but I step in front of her.

"I'm a personal trainer at the gym. My clients are able to work around my schedule, normally," I smile at her, knowing that I just won this round.

"That must be nice. And I'm actually not using sarcasm this time." She rolls her eyes.

"I'm just going to go ahead and ask before I talk myself out of it. Did you want to grab coffee sometime?" I look down at my feet because I'm a coward and can't look her in her eyes.

Silas says, "Dude, she works at a coffee shop. You gotta do better than that." He's right and now I feel stupid. Ash tells her son to go work on his free kicks and then he's off.

"If I'm just a meaningless fuck, then why are you asking me out?" She throws that one back in my face.

"I thought that's what you wanted to hear." Now I feel like a dick.

"Right, because every woman dreams to be some fuck toy. Thank you for clearing that up." She goes to walk past me but I grab her wrist. This conversation is not over.

"No, just the way you were talking it sounded like you didn't want to have any type of meaning behind it. I thought you just wanted to just have sex with somebody and move on. I stepped in because I wanted to make sure you were safe while doing it." I try to explain myself but saying it out loud makes me feel even worse.

"Safe? You didn't want to use a condom. How safe is that?" She exclaims.

"My pull-out game is on point. Plus, I know I'm clean," I say with a smirk.

"You keep thinking that you can just pull out and you will be good to go, you're going to have a big ass family," She responds.

"So, if you don't want coffee, can I take you to breakfast?" I'm grasping at straws at this point.

"If you want to be around me while I'm cranky. I hate mornings." That doesn't surprise me.

"Wait, so you haven't been cranky this whole time?" I start smiling because I know all about the way she interacts at this point. "Okay, lunch then. And if that's a no, I guess we can skip the getting to know each other part and go straight to dinner." I give her a smirk and she starts to blush. I love bringing heat to her cheeks.

"Fine, we can start with breakfast but we are going to keep it quiet. I don't need Silas getting all excited." She looks over at him, watching as he makes shitty shots. We are going to work on that.

"I'm just asking for a date. If it goes well then we can go from there." I assure her.

"Thank you for understanding," she responds and then I hear kids start to walk up.

"For now, can you move? I have practice to start." She smiles up at me and that's when I notice how short she is. She comes up to my chest. Oh, this is going to be fun.

# Chapter 3
## Ash

Jace has been coming to the coffee shop every morning since Thursday. I told him that we had to wait for the weekend that Silas stays with his dad before we go on that breakfast date. There's no need to get him excited if it doesn't work out. It's Saturday and I have the whole day planned out with my baby. I'm going to make us pancakes and then play some video games on his XBOX. He's having his first game tonight so he can't eat a bunch of junk food like we normally do. Sunday we're going to stay in our pajamas and have a *Star Wars* movie marathon with popcorn and Twizzlers. I love our weekends together. Sure I have him during the week but he's in school and I have work. I walk into Silas's room to get him up and going but when I open the door, he's already up and dressed in his practice clothes.

"Hey bud, what are you doing?" I'm so confused.

"I texted Coach Jace and he said he would practice with me this morning. He said if you couldn't take me then he would come get me." He finishes pulling his socks up.

"Okay well, you need to eat breakfast first." I can at least parent him a little bit.

"I already did, had two pieces of toast." He must be excited because he is never up this early on a Saturday.

"Give me a minute to get dressed and I'll take you." Jace being in my house is not a good idea.

"Thanks, Mom. I'll text him and tell him to just meet us there." Welp, there goes my plans for us. But I get it, he's nervous. That's fine because I didn't get Jace's number anyways. I think I'm just going to wait until he asks for mine, I don't want to sound desperate or anything. While getting dressed, I notice that I'm putting extra time into picking out my outfit. Shaking my head, I blindly pick a shirt and get some shorts. I don't really have to pay much attention because all of my clothes match. I don't like crazy colors and my wardrobe is very basic. I head to my mirror and put my makeup on and then brush my hair. What's the point in brushing it if I just throw it up? I think I'm going to keep it down for now. I'll bring my scrunchie because I know I will change my mind soon. Giving myself a once over, I decide that it's as good as it's going to get. I throw on my white socks with red lobsters on them and then my black slip-on Vans. I head out into the living room to tell Silas that I'm ready to leave. When I get there he's standing at the door, looking down to his phone.

"I'm ready to go," I announce.

"It's about time. He's going to be there waiting for us." He's bouncing from one foot to the other.

"Calm down, let me just get my phone and keys. Go ahead to the car." Kids are so impatient. I am not about to rush just to sit and watch him run around for God knows how long. I get in the car and drive in silence to the field. We pull up at the same time as a silver BMW, I assume it's Jace. Silas gets out of the car so fast that you would think his ass was on fire. I grab his water bottle and my phone and walk to the sideline. I really should buy a fold-up chair, or at least remember to bring a blanket to sit on. I don't mind the dirt but after a while, my ass will start to hurt. Nothing that I can do about that now, so I sit and start watching TikTok on my phone. While I'm watching a thirst trap of a man dressed up as a firefighter holding his hose, I feel somebody behind me. I turn my head to see who it is and of course, it's Jace.

"Is that why so many fires go untouched? These guys are prancing around half-naked playing with the water." I exit the app and put my phone down. "You do know that none of that is real? The filters they use are insane." He tries to pop my bubble.

"Do you need something?" I'm slightly irritated by the interruption.

"I noticed that you sit on the ground at every practice so I brought you a chair." He steps to the side and I see a bright orange fold-up chair.

"No sir, I will not sit in that ugly ass thing," his eyes ask the question before it comes out of his mouth. "Do you watch football?"

"Don't you dare say you like those damn chickens." He straightens.

"They are better than being a pussy." It's a staring contest now.

"You can keep your ass on the ground. I don't want you to touch it anyway." I can't help but smile. I'm a South Carolina Gamecock fan but I don't actually care about the color of the chair.

"You know I'm just fucking with you?" My throat lets out a small chuckle.

"You scared me for a minute. I thought you weren't a Clemson fan." He puts his hand on his chest and pushes out a breath.

"Oh, I was dead serious about that. I was talking about the colors. I don't care what color your stuff is." He looks slightly offended.

"We are going to have to figure this out. It's okay, I will make it work." A smile peaks out from his sexy pale lips.

"That must be very hard for you." I squint my eyes and nibble on my lip.

"I guess I'm going to need your number so that we can talk about it." Now that makes me laugh hard.

"That was cute. Very slick. Give me your phone before I change my mind." He unlocks his phone and hands it to me. The background is of the soccer field. It looks like he was standing at the corner facing towards the center of the field. It was taken once the sun started coming up. It's beautiful. I pull up his contacts and add my number. I thought about texting myself to have his number but I think I'll wait until he wants to start talking. "Here ya go. I'm going to steal your chair for today. Now go help my son."

"Yes ma'am." He smiles and then makes his way to Silas. I pull the chair out, grab my phone from off the ground and get comfortable. This is much better than the hard earth. My phone starts to vibrate in my lap so I pick it up to see an unknown number text. I open it up and can't stop myself from smiling.

> **UNKNOWN: Just so you don't have to sit around waiting for my call. Now save my number.**

> **ME: You are very bossy.**

Of course, I immediately program it because I get anxious if I don't see a name and only the number.

> **ASSHAT: Sometimes, but I have my moments.**

> **ME: I'm not obedient.**

> **ASSHAT: That just makes it even more fun.**

> **ME: Shut up and teach my kid how to kick.**

I look up from my phone to see him staring at me. I shake my head because I know this is either going to end really badly or I might actually be happy. Happy... I haven't felt that in a while. They run around for another hour before they stop for a break.

"Silas, it's lunchtime. Let's go!" I yell at him.

"Awe, Mom." He pouts. I can't stand that. "Can Coach eat with us?"

"I'm sure Coach Jace has his own plans." Of course, he has to join our conversation then.

"I don't have anything going on today except the game. Let it be my treat." He winks.

"Absolutely not, I can pay for Silas and myself. I can take care of my family," I snap. I don't need any help.

"Hold on now, I was just talking about lunch. I'm not asking to buy you a house and pay for your hair and nails." He throws his hands up and takes a step back.

"I don't even get my nails done. My hair gets cut once every six months. I wouldn't need your help with that either," I hear the crazy in my voice but I can't stop it.

"Okay then, Silas, I think I'm going to head out. I'll see you tonight." He walks past me with his stuff and heads to his car.

"Wait!" I stop him and then tell Silas to go get in the car. I take a few breaths and then walk over to talk to Jace. "Look, I'm sorry. I'm not used to anybody paying for my stuff. The last man that I was with, he gave me gifts and took me out when he wanted sex," I shamefully admit.

"I'm not trying to get in your pants. I already did that, remember?" His finger touches under my chin and gently moves my face up so that I can look into his eyes. "It was rather nice and I would love to be inside of you again.

The sooner the better. But I'm not going to basically pay you for it. When I take you out or give you gifts, I want nothing in return. And I plan to spoil you as you deserve. I want to make you smile every day." Before I realize what I'm doing, I stand on my tiptoes and throw my arms around his neck. I slam my lips on his and I feel the warmth of his tongue prying my lips apart. I welcome it and the kiss deepens. His hand moves from my chin and slowly runs down my side to my hip. He puts the other on the back of my head, tangling his fingers in my hair. I can feel myself getting wet, so I push my thighs together to relieve some of the pressure.

"So um, can y'all stop eating each other's face and get in the car? I need food." Silas gets back into my car and slams the door.

"Shit. I forgot where we were. I'm so sorry, I got caught up and I shouldn't have done that." I'm so stupid. But he doesn't let go, he places a gentle kiss on my lips once and then pulls back just enough to speak.

"Don't ever apologize for kissing me," he grumbles and his lips touch mine when he moves his mouth. "If he wasn't here right now, I would have you in the back of my BMW with no shorts and your legs spread out so I can taste you." I step back out of his embrace before I rip him apart right here.

"I can't be all over you in front of him. I don't know if he is even okay with this." I try to catch my breath. This is so intense.

"You can keep making excuses, but I bet he doesn't care. He's a guy and he likes me." He smiles just enough to show a sliver of teeth. Fuck, he's hot and he's not even trying.

"Okay. One, I don't need to make excuses, I can just say fuck off. And two, just because you play with him, doesn't mean he likes you." I put my hands on my hip and I know I look like a little brat.

"I do love your mouth. I'm sure I can use it for a thing or two." His tongue darts out to lick his bottom lip while he stares at mine.

"You're such a pig." I puff out some air to try and hide my smile.

"Oink, oink." I shouldn't but I kinda do like the attention. I just shake my head and walk to my car.

"Keep up, if you're buying then it's going to be a nice meal." I don't look behind me to see if he's watching or not, but I put a little swing in my hips just in case. Once we are on the road I glance over at Silas. "Hey, I'm sorry about that. I don't know what came over me. Are you okay?"

"Mom, I'm not a little kid anymore. I know women have needs and I don't really care who you mess with. Well, as long as it's not Dad." That takes me by surprise.

"Excuse me? We are not going to gloss over that. How do you know about these 'needs'?" It comes out louder than I was wanting.

"Like I said, I'm not a kid anymore. Plus, Dad's girlfriend told me." I slam on breaks in the middle of the road, I don't give a damn who is behind me. There are horns going off but they are the last thing on my mind.

"What do you mean? What did that little bitch do?" I try not to talk bad about them but fuck that, she crossed a line.

"Jeeze, calm down. She didn't do anything. She asked if you were going out with anybody so I told her no. She said when you do then let it happen because women want to be held too. She said 'held', but I know what she really meant." Nope, don't say anything. Keep your mouth shut, Ash. Breathe, in and out, in and out. We pull up at the restaurant and park. I rushed out of the car and walked further into the lot, out of earshot. I pull my phone out and dial her number. I only have it because of Silas. After two rings, she answers.

"Hello! Oh, I'm so happy that you finally called me. I was hoping that we could talk about what happened with Layne," she has this annoying bubbly voice.

"I don't give two fucks about him! Do you want to tell me why you are talking about women and their needs to my son?" I don't try to hide my anger.

"Oh, he's at that age now and figured he should know. I was just helping you out in case you ever get somebody else," she actually thinks she did me a favor. That is so sad.

"Excuse the fuck out of me?! Who the fuck do you think you are?!" Jace walks up and asks what's wrong. I just nod him off but he stays right here with me. "Actually don't answer that! Keep your fucking mouth shut around MY son! Know your fucking place bitch because if you talk to Silas about any of that shit again then I will do a hell of a lot more than yell through the phone!" I hear a male voice in the distance on her side.

"Ash, what's the problem? Don't call my girlfriend and start bitchin'," a man says over the phone.

"Go fuck yourself, Layne!" I hang up on him and clench my teeth together, screw my eyes shut, and internally scream. After about a good minute, I ease up and relax my face. Again I breathe, in and out, in and out. I clear my throat and shake the irritation off. Jace is staring at me like I'm crazy.

"Umm, are you good now?" He is very careful with his words.

"Yup. Let's go eat," I clip.

"So your thoughts on a good meal is Arbys?" I smile up at him.

"I guess it doesn't take much to make me happy." I feel my smile growing wider.

"Cheap date, I like it." We both chuckle and walk back to Silas.

# Chapter 4

## Jace

"Alright Gladiators, this is what we've been practicing for. I'm not going to tell you to go out there and have fun. You're not a bunch of girls! We are going to go out there and take everything we got to beat them! Remember, when you are out there, you are a family. You are one and I expect to hear some communication! Now y'all are going to go out there with your bright-ass highlighter yellow shirts and win this first game, yeah?"

The team yelled, "Yes!"

"Now huddle up and put your hands in!" They gather in a circle and throw their hands in the middle.

"Start strong, finish strong! Now go out there and make me proud." They are pumped and the energy out here is on a crazy high. Win or lose, I will make sure they know that I am proud. If they don't suck, that would make it easier for me. They look so good out there. Four on defense, four on mid, two forwards, and of course, my goalie. Sometimes I'll mix up the numbers but this is my go-to set-up.

There's the coin toss and it's their ball. The ref calls out to each goalie to confirm that they are ready and steps back to blow his whistle. One of the boys from the other team kicks the ball to the side toward his teammate. They start to run and spread out, passing the ball back and forth. Luke, one of my forwards, steals the ball and gives it two small kicks. He passes it to the other forward, Danny. They are doing some amazing teamwork.

Passing it four more times, Luke takes a chance with the goal. I'm on my toes trying not to run out there. One of the hardest things about being an ex-soccer player is that you can't step in and join the game. The ball flies to the top right corner and the goalie barely misses it. Luke and Danny jump up and chest bump, they are so excited and I love it. They are setting back up and it's our ball. Luke kicks it back to Charlie, one of my mids. Luke and Danny run ahead and Charlie dribbles it a couple of times and takes a big kick and it goes to Luke. He takes it and tries to get control but his footing is off and the other team takes the ball from us and runs it down the sideline.

"Come on midfield! Where are y'all at? Get it together," I yell out at my team. Ambrose, one of the defensemen, runs up to the guy and rushes him. Making the other team kick it out of bounds. Corner kick. Ambrose lines it up and kicks it up in the air, halfway across the field. The other team hits the ball with their head and Charlie bounces it off of his knee. Danny is right there with the ball and gets it under control. He passes it to Luke and he takes the shot. The ball goes to the lower left and the goalie throws himself on the ground, catching the ball. Without pausing, the goalie gets up, runs to his line, and punts it. The ball goes down the field and to the right. Pierce, my other mid, gets behind it and runs it down the sideline. He's got a player from the other team running beside him, trying to get Pierce to throw the ball away.

"Pierce! Pass the ball! Pass it!" I hear Luke telling him to pass it to him. Pierce slows down and rolls the ball under his foot to get behind the other player. He goes behind the other player and kicks it to Luke. He runs it to the goal but passes it to Danny fast and Danny makes the goal.

"Yes! That's how we do it! Teamwork!" I cheer.

The rest of the game goes by pretty fast. The other team got two goals and we won with five. I line the boys up and we all cross the field, touching hands with the other team. When the coach gets to me, we shake hands and say good game. Heading back to the bench where all of my team is jumping up and down together, I can't drop the smile that I have plastered on my face. I'm glad that I got Ash to order some pizza because I am starving. Another parent brought a cooler full of Gatorade.

"Guys, gather around and take a knee," I call out to them. They are still pumped and hurry over to me. "That was a great first game. I have absolutely nothing negative to say. The teamwork out there was phenomenal. I am so proud of y'all. But don't let this win get to your heads. Just because this game was great, doesn't mean next week's game will be that good. Keep your head on your shoulders. Come on, get up and put your hands in the middle." Once we are all together in a circle, I yell out, "What do we say?!"

"Start strong, finish strong!" They all say together.

"Good, now go eat," I tell them. I am damn proud.

The team did a great job, pizza is well deserved. What takes me by surprise is when I see that same mom from the first practice handing everybody a slice. Can they not all grab their own? She looks up at me and she has this smile that doesn't mean anything good. Ash is watching and she starts to laugh. Why is she laughing? I can understand her smiling at the situation but I don't think it's that funny. I look back to the mom and I see why Ash is having a grand ol' time over there. The lady is walking to me, playing with her fingers.

"Hey there, Coach. That was some game the boys played. You must work very hard." Her eyes travel my body.

"No ma'am, that game was all them." She puts one hand on my arm and squeezes, this is starting to get a little awkward. I look to the side to find Ash laughing so hard that she almost falls out of her seat. I'm glad somebody is loving this.

"You don't have to call me ma'am. My name is Darla. If you need anything, anything at all, let me know. Can I see your phone to put my number in?" She asks but that's going to be a big no.

"I don't have my phone on me during games, ma'am." That was a lie and I made sure not to say her name.

"Oh, well wait right here and I will get some paper for you to write it down. I'll be right back." Once she walks away, I make eye contact with Ash. Pleading for her to come help. We haven't gone on that first date yet but we have been spending a lot of time together. Silas is always there, but still. Neither of us has talked about labels but she can at least see that I don't want to be here, right? To my luck, she picks up on the question in my eyes and walks over here.

"Help," I beg.

"What? You don't want that? She seems like a catch." Her sarcasm has no limits.

"It's a good thing I don't have a ball to throw." I try to be funny.

"So you don't have balls? That does make sense because if you had them, you would have told her you weren't interested. Unless you are, and in that case, I will go sit back down." She takes a step back.

"You know I only have interest in you." This isn't how I wanted to ask her but I'm going to take the opportunity. "You are already my girlfriend, so why would I need her entertainment?" Okay, so that wasn't actually asking but I got my point across. Some parents walk up, interrupting us.

"That was a good game, Coach," one mom says.

"It was a team effort," I tell them. I get lucky and they don't want to have a full-on conversation, so they walk away.

"Girlfriend? Wow, you assume that I like you." She picks our talk back up.

"Well I mean, I was hoping you did. If you don't, can you just feel sorry for me and be mine anyways?" Smooth, real smooth. Idiot.

"Hmmm." She gets closer to me and puts her hands just below my chest and stands on her toes. I lean in and we kiss. Not a punishing or needy kiss. Just a small peck to show everybody that I am off-limits. The kiss is over almost right as it started. I want more but I don't think the kids want to see that. The parents might, but I'm not one to share. "You are going to have to ask me properly." She smiles up at me, waiting.

"Will you be my girlfriend?" I don't realize I'm holding my breath until she pulls me down to whisper in my ear.

"No. When you ask, I want you to be inside of me so I can moan out a yes." My mouth opens slightly and I close my eyes. This girl is going to get me in so much trouble. I can't wait to see what rules we break. My dick gets hard almost immediately.

"Good job, now you're going to have to stand in front of me for the rest of this. I'm always the last to leave, so you will be here for a while. My gym shorts won't do anything to hide this." I spin her around so that her ass is pushing against my hardness and I hear a little moan escape her mouth. "If I have to suffer, so do you." She wiggles her hips to make a bit of friction. The things I am going to do to this woman when I take her to bed.

I look up and immediately lock eyes with Darla.

"Okay, she saw us. I think she might be upset," I forgot all about that mom. I see Silas walking up to us and I try to straighten myself out.

"Can I go over to Colton's house to play some video games?" Silas asks Ash.

"Did his mom say that it was okay?" Ash asks in return.

"Yeah, she said she can drive me home too." He is hopping from one foot to the other.

"That's fine but don't eat a bunch of junk," she tells him.

"Sure Mom," he lies. That's probably all he will be eating.

"I love you, be safe," Ash tells him and a small part of me wants her to use those same words on me.

"I love you too." He runs off to his friend and I have the biggest smile on my face.

"Do you know what that means, Ash?" I whisper in her ear.

"Yeah, that means I can go home and take a hot bubble bath." She wiggles her ass again and hums.

"Actually, I was thinking that I could take you home. Or to my house. I don't really care either way." I just want the teasing to stop and her moaning out my name.

"Who said I want to sleep with you?" She raises a brow in question.

"I never said anything about sleeping. I was thinking about taking care of that smart mouth of yours."
A couple of the boys walk up with their parents, interrupting us once again.

"See ya', Coach." They wave as they walk away.

"Y'all did a great job out there. Bring that same energy to practice Monday," I tell them.

"Are you okay, man?" Somebody's dad asks.

"Oh, yeah I'm all good. Ash here is just helping me stay up. I don't want to fall over." Thinking on my feet. Ash starts snickering.

"Okay, well, that was a great game. Y'all have a good night." The dad nods.

"You too, man," I call back.

"You have way too much confidence. You haven't taken me out or anything and you think I'm going to go ahead and give you dessert?" She's cute when she plays hard to get.

"Are you hungry? I can feed you first but I want my dessert." I lean down to her neck and lick.

"Let me ask Colton's mom if Silas can stay the night," her voice is breathy.

"Wow, I tell you that I will feed you and you invite yourself over for the night." I put my hand on my chest to look astonished.

"Shut up. You talk so much game, now let's see if you can live up to it." I watch her ass as she walks to the group of parents. Her shorts are loose but still show off her curves. I've always been an ass man, lucky for me she has the perfect one. I can't wait to make it pink. These black gym shorts do nothing to hide the bulge. I can't pull my jersey down to help it either so I try to hide it with my hands. She better hurry up or I'm going to have to hide in my car. Most of the kids are gone but I still won't leave until they all do. Finally, she's coming back, laughing about something.

"That took forever," I sigh.

"What's the rush, you won't be leaving right away?" She looks around at the kids.

"I'm not rushing to leave. I just need you to stand in front of me and hide what you've done." I talk to her like she's a child in trouble.

"What I've done? You started it!" She pushes at my chest and she is surprisingly strong. I have to take a couple of steps back.

"Okay, I did not expect that from a tiny person." I smile with shock.

"Expect what?" I grab her arm and check out her muscles. "Oh that, yeah I have to lift boxes of coffee a lot. I guess I could call it my own little workout, but that is as far as it goes."

"Do you run or do yoga?" There are so many things that I still don't know about her and I'm itching for more.

"If you see me running, you better start too because there must be a fire. As far as yoga goes, I get bored with it, and anyway, I'm at the coffee shop a lot." She shrugs her shoulders. Still holding on to her arm, I pull her to me and spin her to face out.

"Well, we will just have to figure out some way to get your cardio in," I tell her as I give a quick kiss on her neck. She grinds her ass into me again. "Keep it up and we won't make it to dinner."

"If you are taking me out, would that be considered a date?" She asks as she leans back on me.

"Do you want it to be?" I wrap my arms around her.

"That's not what I asked," her voice has a slight irritation in it. She isn't playing around or making small talk anymore.

"I would like for it to count as one but I'll enjoy it no matter what you want to label it as." I don't want to come off as controlling so I want her to have the option. I can't fuck this up.

"All jokes aside, are you wanting to get to know me or do you just want to hook up?" How could she even question that? She stiffens in my arms.

"I can go anywhere for a hookup, I want to know you. I want to know your likes and dislikes, the first thing you do when you get out of bed and the last thing you do before you get back in. I want to know how you take your coffee and your favorite non-coffee drink. I want to know you." She doesn't say anything for a minute so I turn her around to look into her eyes. They are glassy and I'm starting to think that nobody has wanted her, for her. The men in her past, no, the boys in her past weren't shit.

Out of the corner of my eyes, I see parents walking up but I hold up a finger to tell them to hang on in the nicest way I can. This is a conversation that needs to happen and not be put off. My focus goes back to Ash.

"Pee, take my medicine, creamer with a splash of coffee and Dr. Pepper." It takes me a moment but I catch on. That's her answer.

"Creamer with a splash of coffee?" I ask her with a smile. That makes her smile.

"Yes, I own a coffee joint and I don't really like coffee. That just helps the inventory." I'm still not understanding. She must see it on my face because then she explains further. "I really like the smell of the coffee beans. I will drink the frappes but there's hardly any coffee in there. I'm rarely behind the register anyways. I'm better at running the business. I can do all of the financial things, I really like making the space pretty and I can market the shit out of it too. I just need help with telling people what's good."

"The place does look nice." I try to get her to smile a little more.

"I'm wanting to change some things. Make it cozier." She looks around and crosses her arms.

"What were you thinking?" I ask while I take her into my arms and pull her back to me.

"Maybe on the right side of the store, take the tables and chairs out. Replace them with couches and soft chairs and a small... more to the ground... table," she describes her vision to me and I want to help.

"Like a coffee table?" I raise my eyebrows and smile.

"Yes asshat, a coffee table." What the hell did she just say?

"I'm sorry, asshat?" I move my hands up to cup her face.

"That's what I call you behind your back." She has this smile that says she loves my reaction.

"Okay, but why?" I chuckle because she's so fucking cute. I let go of her face so that she can talk.

"When we met, you interrupted mine and the bartender's conversation with your cockiness. And then you called me a meaningless fuck. So, asshat." Ah, yeah we gotta clear that one up real fast.

"I didn't mean what I said, it was not meaningless. We both definitely came. So there was meaning." Her pretty pink lips start to separate and I take the advantage and lean down to kiss her. Instead of participating, she starts slapping me on my arm. I break our one-sided kiss and give her a little smile. "I'm just kidding. If the bar didn't happen then we wouldn't be this close. Or at least not this early in the season."

"Carry-on." Her hands are on her hips and my mouth starts to water. I can see her curves just a little more with the way her hand dips. I put my hands on either side of her waist and pulled her in. Leaning down, my lips get so close to her ear that if she moved the slightest, I would be biting down on it. I take a second to inhale her smell. Coconut with some sweetness, it's addictive.

"If we didn't meet in that bar, then right now I would be watching you from a distance. Staring at those long, creamy, perfect legs. Wondering how good you would taste if I bite down on that round apple ass. Maybe I would have thought about pulling this long, deep chocolate hair. But then I would have gone home after every practice and game, thinking about what it would sound like when you moan out my name because I'm deep inside you. Luckily for me, we did meet. Now I go home and think all of those things plus I think about how you taste when my tongue is playing in your mouth. Now, I can hold you." Stretching my arms around her, I grab a handful of that juicy ass. "Now, I can grab one of my favorite parts of you."

I pull my face back to where I am looking into her eyes. They have darkened. But then I step away, I want her to know that I want more than that, so I change the way the conversation was going. "Now that we did meet in that bar, I can sit with you on your couch and watch movies. Go to a gas station to get Freezies and see who can drink it the fastest without getting a brain freeze. Maybe even hold each other's hand while skydiving." Her face went ghostly white.

"Fuck no." Oh, she's serious. Good thing, I don't like heights.

"No skydiving. Noted. I am looking forward to all of the things that we get to do together." I look around to see how many people are still here. I usually don't mind them hanging out but damn, go home already.

"I'm not even your girlfriend yet and you are thinking about all these things." Her eyebrows scrunch up and between them makes a little V. It's kinda cute.

"I know what I want when I see it. We have talked every morning at your work for the last three days and earlier I got to talk to you and your son for five hours. I would know by now if this wasn't something that I was interested in. And here I am, interested. If you want to take things slow, we can. But just know, at whatever speed, I will still be here, smartass." We both chuckle. "I might be an asshat, but you are my smartass." Her smile is the sexiest thing I have ever seen. Her teeth are white, but not fake white, and straight except for one tooth. Her top left canine is slightly turned outward. Breaking our little bubble, she looks around. One parent is still waiting to talk, not sure where the others went.

"Hey, sorry about that. What's going on," I ask the tall dad that is incredibly built. *I wonder if he goes to my gym. I will have to keep a lookout.*

"It is what it is. I just wanted to introduce myself. I'm Tyler and I can help out with the boys if you need it," he says a bit snarky.

"Thanks, man. I will definitely take you up on that offer," I respond with what I hope was very calm. He looks over at Ash and nods his head once, then he's gone. I blow out a puff of air and head back to my girl.

"It seems everybody left and we didn't even notice. I guess I'll head home now," she says and it takes me off guard because I just saw kids here not even ten minutes ago.

"Okay, if you don't want to hang out tonight then it's alright." Her face scrunches up again and she looks confused.

"I still want to, if the offer stands. But I am not going anywhere with you while you smell like that. You stink. Go take a shower." She takes a step back. I lift my arm up to make a show of it and take a deep whiff. I start coughing and she starts laughing.

"I guess I can do that. I brought clothes to change into because I was going to shower at the gym, but I guess I'll go home instead. Get all hot for you." Winking and earning a headshake.

"Why would you shower at the gym anyways?" She asks, confused.

"Makes it easier for me to go get food afterward. If I go home to shower, I won't leave and would just eat cereal for dinner." It's pretty much a nightly routine now.

"Or you can just follow me to my house and shower." My eyes go straight to her lips. They are barely parted and her teeth are sinking deep into one side of her bottom lip. It takes all I got to say no but I have to do it.

"I promised to feed you. So I am going to get in my car and drive home, take a cold shower, and dress in something decent. Be ready for this because as a first date, I will not be taking you to a drive-thru." I dread every word. I want to tell her to lead the way and go home to shower with her. To get her naked and wet.

"I'm not really into fancy places." She scrunches up her nose.

"Don't you worry your pretty little head, I know the perfect place." This town doesn't even have super fancy anyways.

"Okay, but I hope it doesn't disappoint." She leaves me there watching as she gets in her car and drives off. When I know that she can't see me anymore, I pump my fist in the air like I just won the damn lottery. I hurry to my car and head home. I'm so excited that I can't stay still. Tapping on my steering wheel, hopping in my seat. It feels like it takes a lot longer than it actually does to get home. I'm thankful that she doesn't like fancy because I have never been to anything five-star.

Once I walk into my house, I go to take a shower. It was quick but thorough. I remember that she likes to overthink so I run over to my phone and text her what to wear.

# Chapter 5
## Ash

**ASSHAT: Jeans and a t-shirt.**

Thank God! I feel like the world has been lifted off of my shoulders. Okay, that may be a little dramatic but I was stressing. I'm standing by my bed with a towel wrapped around me and another wrapped in my wet hair. Most of my clothes are spread out in front of me. I'm stoked that I can wear my basics because I really have nothing else. But then I think of something else, is he picking me up or am I meeting him there? We didn't talk about that part. He doesn't know where I live but I also don't know where to meet him. Life is hard. You know what, it's okay. I'll just text him, that's what the phone is for.

> **ME: I fully expect you to pick me up and if you beep your car horn then you will be going on a date by your lonesome.**

He doesn't respond right away so I go ahead and throw on some black jeans and a beige t-shirt with gray mountains over the chest. I take my hair out of the towel and run a brush through it. It should dry pretty fast. Now for the makeup. I don't want to overdo it but I have to do something with my eyes. If I don't then I'll look half asleep all night. A little cat eye and some mascara, that'll do it. Moving on to my teeth, I'm about to squeeze out toothpaste when my phone dings.

> **ASSHAT: I wouldn't dream of anything else. What's your address?**

I type it out and hit send. Heading back to brush my teeth, my phone dings again.

> **ASSHAT: I'll be there in five minutes. I hope you're ready for this.**

> **ME: That's some big talk.**

How is he so close already?! Scrambling around, I throw on my socks and hurry for my Vans. These damn laces! *KNOCK KNOCK* Shit! Okay, calm down. In and out, in and out. You can do this. I give myself one more minute to get it together and then open the door. Damn, he looks good. Black Adidas, light blue jeans, and a plain black t-shirt. His dark hair is messy, like he's been running his fingers through it. Those ocean-blue eyes have my knees weak.

"I didn't honk," he says.

"I just need to grab my purse. Stay." I point my finger at him.

"Do you want me to sit too?" I ignore him and do my checklist in my mind. Keys, phone, condom, pepper spray, and gum. I think I'll bring chapstick too. Alright, that's it, let's do this thing. He hasn't moved, so I pat his head.

"Good boy." I start walking towards his car with him close behind me.

"Be careful, you don't know what you're asking for with that," he growls in my ear.

"Are you saying that you like to be praised?" I'm shocked, I've never met a man that is into that.

"Try it and find out." Holy fucking shit. Why do I like that so much?

"I will keep that in mind. So where are we going?" I want to know more about his kinks but I'm starving.

"You will see. It's my take on 'nice'." He opens my door and I get in. My nerves are actually not as bad as it was in the house. Something about him eases my mind. His car has this clean smell, I can't put my finger on it but I know it. When he gets in, I can't help myself.

"What's that smell?" I burst out.

"Is it bad?" He looks a bit nervous.

"No, it's nice but what is it?" Still trying to figure it out.

"Don't laugh." He looks down at his thighs.

"Oh, it's guaranteed that I will now." I'm not going to lie. It must be funny if he has to warn me.

"Febreze. The car smelled like dirty socks." Okay, that is actually a good idea though.

"Dirty socks?" I can't see that from him.

"I work at a gym and I coach a sport. It's going to smell bad, but I tried to cover it up." He shrugs his shoulders while he explains.

"Does your house smell like a gym trainer and soccer coach lives there?" That may have been a rude question but it slipped out and I can't take it back now.

"Okay but listen, it's not that bad." He looks at me with a small smile.

"I'm scared." I lean towards the window and put my hand on the door.

"If you don't want to go there after dinner, that's fine. I have no expectations for tonight." I am so fucking with him throughout dinner. This will be fun.

"Now that it's all out in the open, can we go now? I'm impatient." He does that sexy smirk that has been making me feel things.

"Yes, ma'am." He starts driving and his hand goes to rest on my thigh. That little gesture means more than it should to me. I watch his hand for a minute and I try to hide my smile.

"Oh, sorry." He moves it to the steering wheel. I reach over and pull his hand back to my leg.

"This is where it belongs and don't ever move it again." That earns me a full-on smile showing off his perfectly white teeth. The rest of the drive was quiet, but not awkward. We pull into the parking lot of Cracker Barrel.

"Seriously?" Is it bad that I actually love this?

"Yup. I love this place." At this point, I have to laugh. I make myself stop because his face looks offended.

"I love it. It is pretty fancy though. High class for me." I take my seatbelt off and look back at him.

"You don't have to make fun of me," he says in a hurt tone. Oh no.

"I'm not. I am actually being very serious. I was laughing because I'm relieved. The past couple of hours I've been so worried that you planned to take me to someplace that served plates with two bites' worth of food on them. I'm happy to be here." Thankfully, his smile comes back. I lean over the console and give him a quick peck on his lips. We sit there for a minute just staring at each other. My stomach growls and messes up the moment.

Embarrassed I get out of the car. We meet at the front and I take his hand in mine, then head to the restaurant doors. Normally I would be scared to hold a guy's hand for the first time but everything feels so natural with him. We have only been talking for a week and I'm already having feelings for him. I know it's too soon but I want a future with him. He makes me feel good. The hostess shows us to our table and I try to pull my chair out but Jace beats me to it.

"Come on now, there's no way you didn't see this happening," he says as I gape.

"I just don't want to assume something will happen and then get disappointed when it doesn't." I want him to know where the bar is set.

"Always assume with me. If I disappoint you, call me out on it. I don't want to slack off," he says seriously.

"I will try my best." We get settled in and the waitress comes over. I order water and Jace orders tea. I really didn't want water but I felt like I had to because it doesn't cost anything. We look over our menus and I go straight for the prices. If he's paying then I want to get something pretty cheap. They have a daily dinner special and today is their country-fried pork chop. That actually sounds good. On the side, I'm thinking fresh fruit and dumplings. I eat fruit every chance I can. It's refreshing and it just makes me feel good.

The waitress comes back with our drinks and we order our food. I expect the awkward small talk but it never comes. The conversation just flows and I catch myself actually enjoying this. We talk about Silas and what happened with his dad. I tell him about my trust issues and my anxiety, I go ahead and get the fact that I'm on medication out of the way. He tells me about his work and how his ex cheated on him too. After all the deep talk, I decide to move on to lighter questions.

"So, what's your favorite color?" I start with the basics.

"Purple. Yours?" He says.

"Really? That's Silas's favorite too. Mine is teal. I will literally buy anything if it's that color." I'm not stretching the truth either, everything is in teal.

"That's good to know. What hobby do you have?" He asks.

"I hardly ever have time for myself, much less a hobby. But the rare times that I do get downtime, I enjoy reading." I like that it takes me to another world.

"That's interesting. What do you like to read about?" He is going to regret that question.

"My go-to is fantasy. I love reading about a world that doesn't exist but I also love some good romance. The dirtier the better." I go ahead and put my inner slut out there.

"I will try and live up to whatever is in those books. I like to rock paint." That catches me off guard.

"Rock paint?" Did I hear that right?

"Yeah, like rocks about the size of your hand and smooth. I like to paint them. Not just one color, I paint pictures." His eyes light up when he explains it.

"That is actually pretty cool. I didn't know you were an artist." I can imagine his house filled with rocks.

"I wouldn't say I'm an artist but I try." Our food shows up and we start to eat. Halfway through our meal, I start to fuck with him.

"This is so good, mmm." I let out a small moan and roll my eyes back. He just stares at me. I start picking up my strawberries and orange slices and suck them into my mouth, letting the juices run down my chin. "Oops, sorry, sometimes I get a little messy." He squirms a little in his seat and I pretend I don't notice. I clean my mouth off with my finger and stick it in my mouth to suck it off.

I sit back in my chair like nothing happened. "Thank you for dinner, it was a good pick."

"I'm glad you…" I start running my foot up his leg and onto his thigh. He struggles with his words when my shoe starts rubbing against the now hardness in his pants. "…enjoyed your…umm… your food." He drops his head and closes his eyes. Turning him on is actually turning me on. I love that I can make him feel like this with hardly any effort. The waitress comes over with the check but I don't stop. It's all under the table so she can't see anything. Jace does a good job of acting like nothing is happening. "You are about to be in so much trouble," he tells me.

"Oh no, I'm so scared." The sarcasm was hard to keep inside. I drop my foot and stand after he pays. Watching him stand and try to hide himself is entertaining enough. There is tension on the walk back to the car but I fully expect it. We get there and he opens my door, I can't stop myself now. I boop his nose. "Good boy." I try to get into his but he grabs my arm and walks me back onto it. His mouth is on mine before I catch up on what's happening. His lips move to my jaw and then he runs his mouth down to my neck. He gently kisses and then licks.

"I want to bite you but right now, I would leave a mark and I'm sure you don't want that. But I need to know right now, where are we going?" His voice is low.

"I was hoping we could go to your house and you could get around to asking me to be your girlfriend." That's all he needed because he picked me up bridal style and put me in my seat, buckling my belt for me. Once he's in the car, he speeds off. His hand goes to my thigh and squeezes. I can't hold back the moan that slips out. I think I heard him growl but I might be hearing things because I'm so aroused that I'm not thinking about anything other than that hand moving up my thigh.

"How much further is your house?" I need to be on him.

"Right around this corner." He seems a little more composed than I would like. Is he starting to regret this? Maybe I should tone it down. He might have just realized he doesn't want to do this. I'll just have to push these feelings to the side, I don't want to come off as desperate. He pulls up to this nice, big, one-story brick house. There are some rocking chairs on the front porch and plants hanging from the roof. His yard is so big compared to mine. There's no way he lives here by himself.

"Wow. Is anybody home?" I ask.

"I mean, there is now. I live by myself." He stares at me like he's contemplating something.

"Sorry, it's just big. I would think more people would be here." It's enough to hold an entire family.

"Nope, just me. I'll tell you the story behind it another time." He gets out and walks around to open my door. We hold hands going up the walkway to the front porch. "Are you okay?" I didn't notice I was fidgeting with my nails.

"Yeah, I just get nervous in new places," my voice comes out shaky.

"Are you sure you want to come in? We can go." He takes a step back allowing me to walk away.

"I mean, only if you want to. I don't mind if we stay." I'm embarrassed now. I wish I wasn't like this.

"What's on your mind? Open up to me." I wish he would just unlock the door and drop the conversation. I don't like talking about feelings.

"I just don't want you to feel like you have to do anything now that we are here." I can't meet his eyes so I look down at my shoes.

"What would make you think that I don't want to?" His finger is under my chin and he lifts my face to look at him.

"You haven't jumped on me yet or anything." He actually starts laughing. Is he seriously laughing at me? I make a move to walk away but he steps in front of me.

"Do you think it's easy for me to not bend you over right now? I wanted you to make the first move because I don't want you to think that's why we are here. I just want to spend time and get to know you more." That's all I needed to hear. I push him to his door, wrap my fingers in his hair and then devour his mouth.

# Chapter 6

# Jace

I love the taste of her. I sink my teeth in her bottom lip and pull. She starts to pull my hair and I bend down to grab the underside of her thighs and lift her up. She wraps her legs around me and I turn us to walk her to my door.

"Hold on to me." I get the keys out of my pocket without breaking the kiss. I try to unlock the door but I can't think straight with her tongue playing with mine… I force myself off her mouth and she licks up my neck. I get the door unlocked and open when she bites me. "Fuck." I have never needed somebody this bad before. I'm going to take my time on her this go-round. My lips slam back onto hers and my tongue pries hers apart. She allows me entrance and our tongues do a little dance.

Attempting to walk through the single-story layout of the house to get to my bedroom without breaking contact, I use my foot to slam the front door closed. Or at least I try to but then she pulls her tongue out of my mouth and bites down on my bottom lip. I slam us into the wall of the entranceway a little more forcefully than I intended. It doesn't seem to bother her because she starts tugging at my hair again. I nip her jaw and then her neck. Her head falls back to the wall with a thud. Her breathing picks up and she starts wiggling her hips to have some kind of friction. I push myself onto her harder so that she can't move. "No ma'am. I'm the only one that gets to make you cum."

Her lips come down to my ear and she whispers, "Be a good boy and fuck me."

She's figured out how to get her way. I walk her to my bed. Throw her down and take my shirt off. Her eyes scan my abs with hunger. She moves to the edge of the bed and places her hands on my sides. I watch her as she licks my stomach. "You taste good but I bet other parts of you taste better." She's not going to get that chance this time. I push her back on the bed to where she's laying down. Her hair is fanned out over my gray comforter, her eyes are dark, she's biting her already swollen lips and I can see the pebbles of her nipples and her piercings. I take my time removing her shoes and socks. She tries to undo her pants but I pop her hand. This is my show, she just needs to lay there.

I sink to my knees and slowly move my mouth to her lower thigh and give her love bites. She starts to squirm and breathe loudly. I nip her other thigh and I'm rewarded with a low moan I can barely hear. I go back and forth, working my way up to her sweet center. I hold her hips down in an attempt to keep her still. My mouth goes to where the seams come together on her jeans and I push my tongue as hard as I can onto her. I'm watching her as she scrunches her eyes close and bites her lip so hard that I'm surprised I don't see blood. This is driving her crazy and I love it. I pull back and take her pants off. Holy fucking shit. She's bare. No panties and she's shaved. Ignoring my hard dick which is now getting painful while it pushes against my zipper, I dive in. My hands hold her thighs open and I lick from her entrance to clit once. I don't try to hold my moan in.

"You taste fucking delicious." I take my time eating her because damn, I fucking love it. I push my tongue into her entrance and pull it out, just to push it back in. Her moans are becoming louder and it's addictive. I start to lick her again and push two fingers into her slowly. Fuck she's tight. I pull out and push back in, over and over. I continue to lick her perfect pussy for the next minute but I have to be inside of her. I turn my fingers that are inside her into a hook and stroke her G-Spot while I lick and suck the bead that makes her lose it. Her legs go tight around my head and her back arches off the bed. Her moans are loud as she chants, "fuck, fuck, fuck." Her hands find my head and she pushes my face into her even more. I just found my drug and I have no intentions of giving it up. Her legs fall and she lets go of my head. I lick her slowly trying to draw every bit of orgasm left in her. When she starts to smile, I pull my fingers out and stand up. Making sure she is looking at me, I stick my fingers in my mouth and suck her juices off. She sits up but I push her back down. "My house, I'm in charge."

"You look so good when you take over like that," she praises. I can't go slow anymore, I have to feel her tightness sucking me in. I rip her shirt off and unhook her silk bra, and toss it onto the floor. I take a minute to admire her sexy curves. Fuck me. I unbutton my pants and pull them and my briefs off. I put one knee on the bed and she stops me.

"You know the rule." Condom, right. Luckily I bought a box the Saturday after I met her. I had no idea if I would run into her again but I wanted to be prepared if I came across that problem again. I get up and walk to my bedside table. Get one out of the drawer, tear it open with my teeth, and roll it on. I crawl onto the bed and get between her legs. I hold my dick and line it up to her entrance. I push the head in and back out. Then in a little deeper and lean down and take her nipple between my teeth. I lightly bite, suck and lick. I switch to the other and do the same. *We can't have one feeling left out.* I pull back a little and look into her eyes. I give her a smirk, then sink all the way in. Her eyes roll back, her breath hitches, and I stay still for a minute so that she can adjust to me. Damn, she feels like heaven. I remember she felt good at the bar but this is different. This is even better. When her breathing starts to slow down, I start to move. Her hands fly to my back and with each thrust, her nails dig a little deeper.

"You feel so good," she moans. She makes me feel amazing. I almost forgot what I'm here for.

"Tell me." She tries to speak but she doesn't stop moaning. "Say it," I command.

"Say what?" She manages to finally respond.

"Tell me that you're mine," I pant and lick her jaw, waiting.

"That's not going to do it. Try again." She smiles and forces it out. Okay, she wants to play, I can play. I sit up on my knees and pull out of her. She goes to say something but stops when I grab her wrist and ankle, flipping her over. I pull her ass up so that she is on her knees. She tries to sit all the way up but I push her shoulders down to the mattress. I thrust myself inside her and stay still.

"Whose are you?" I try again.

"Nobodys." I slap her right cheek and then rub the sting out.

"Whose are you?" She takes a second to think.

"Nobodys." I slap her left cheek but let it sting for a moment before I rub it.

"Don't be a smart ass. Let's try this again. Whose girlfriend are you?" I ask for the last time.

"Yours." Finally. I start thrusting into her again, fast. "Fuck, fuck, yes. Stop." I immediately stop what I'm doing and pull out.

"What's wrong? What happened?" I hope I didn't hurt her. Damnit, I shouldn't have gone that hard.

"It's my turn to be on top." She gets up and I lay on my back.

"Maybe we should come up with some kind of safeword." I let out a breath, relieved.

"Why would we need that? Are you into some crazy stuff?" She smiles and wiggles her eyebrows.

"No, but next time you say stop, I won't have a heart attack," I explain to her. I honestly was scared.

"Oh, I'm sorry. But now that we got that straight, I'm going to saddle up and ride you."

She straddles me and sinks down on my dick. Her warmth sucks me in and I'm flying. I grab her waist and she starts rolling her hips. She slides her hands up and down my abs. "Show me what you like." I'm a little nervous because not everybody is okay with it, but I have to try. I take her hand and run it up my chest to my neck.

"Don't squeeze hard, just a little pressure." I hold my breath waiting for her reaction. She grabs on and smiles. Slowly she starts to move again. I dig into her sides and help her move faster. Her moans get louder while her other hand scratches my chest. I try not to cum but fuck, she looks so good riding me. Her nipples are hard, her eyes are closed and her tight pussy is grabbing onto my dick and sucking it without mercy. I feel her tightening around my shaft, she's close. She opens her eyes and looks at me.

"You look so good under me. Cum for me baby." She tightens her hold on my neck and she starts to cum. "Fuck, Jace." I cum so hard that I see stars. She moves her hand away from my throat and sits still for a minute then rolls off of me. "Holy shit."

"Yeah. We are doing that again," we both started laughing. After a few minutes of trying to catch my breath, I start noticing the stickiness on my body from the sweat. "I think we need a shower."

She starts giggling and says, "I think you are right."

I get out of bed and take her with me. I throw her over my shoulder and she squeals. I walk to the bathroom while she laughs.

"What are you doing!? It is a nice view of this fine ass!" She starts slapping me and then bites hard.

"Ouch!" I slap her ass back. "Haven't you heard that it's not nice to bite people?"

"I've heard lots of things. I also don't listen." I sit her down on the sink counter and walk over to turn on the shower. I take the condom off, tie it and throw it in the trash can. I walk back over to her and stand between her legs. She wraps them around me and crosses her ankles. I give her a quick peck, then she grabs the back of my neck and pulls me to her mouth. She deepens the kiss and my hands go to her thighs. I pull away and let out a low growl. I take her hand and put it on my dick.

"Do you see what you do to me? You are driving me insane. I feel like a crazed teenage boy," that makes her giggle.

She uses her other hand to grab mine and put it on her pussy. "So what does that make me?" I close my eyes and hang my head. My fingers slide between her folds and push inside of her. She is so wet. I take my hand away and bend down to lick her sweetness.

"Fucking addictive." I stand up and go to pick her up but she pushes me away. She hops off the counter and walks past me to the shower. I turn to watch her round-naked ass. She steps in under the water and I can't make my feet move. I stare as the water cascades down her body. My eyes follow the stream of it. Running through her hair, down the arch of her back, and then showing how thick her ass really is. The water clings to her skin as it makes its way under her ass and circles her legs. I didn't realize I was stroking myself until she looks down at me and licks her lips. I let go of myself and walk into the shower. We are facing each other and I wrap my arms around her waist. Her hands go up to my chest. She looks up and smirks. "What?" I ask her.

"I'm wet," she says and I smile back at her.

"Do you want me to lick it all up for you?" She takes a step back and I thought I said something wrong but then she drops to her knees.

"I would rather lick you right now." She holds my hardened length in one hand and puts her other on my thigh. She licks from the base to the tip, and when she gets there, she circles the head with her tongue. I hold her hair back so that I can see everything she's doing. She puts me in her mouth and I expect her to stop after half was on her tongue, but she takes all of me. Hitting the back of her throat, she starts to gag. I try not to move but when she keeps taking me like this, I can't help but to start pushing her head, quickening her movements. The water hitting her face is mixing with the tears and she looks like a beautiful mess.

"Fuck yes, just like that." I take a sharp breath while she is looking into my eyes.

"I'm about to cum," I warn her. She takes me out of her mouth with a pop.

"Ten points if you can shoot it to the back of my throat." Then she takes me in her mouth again. I have never been with a girl that swallows. I get overly excited and pour myself into her mouth.

"Fuck, Ash. Holy shit," I grunt. She swallows me down and licks the tip to get everything.

"Mmmm, delicious." She licks her lips and then smiles up at me. I help her to her feet and move in to kiss her. She turns away when I get close and grabs my loofa. Squirts some soap onto it and glide it over my body. Once she is satisfied with her cleaning, she gets more soap and washes herself.

"Here, let me do that," I say with some raspiness in my tone.

"No, that's okay. I actually would like to make it out of the shower before the water gets cold." She smirks. I'm about to tell her what every hardworking woman wants to hear. I lean down to her ear and whisper, "My water heater is tankless." I nip her ear and she lets out a low moan. "Oh yes baby, I have it all," that makes her giggle.

"I will definitely keep that in mind but for now, I want to get out," she whispers the last part.

I put my hands up in a defensive gesture. "Okay, okay. I hear you." I smile so that she knows I'm only playing around. After we are finished, dried off, and to my objection, dressed, we sit on the couch.

"I think I need more food," she groans.

"We worked up an appetite," I said and she smiles, sleepily. "What do you want to eat?"

She jumps up and walks to the fridge. "Umm, where's your food?" She asks, shocked.

"I don't see the point in cooking for just me. So I usually just eat out," I tell her as a matter of factly.

She looks disgusted. "I can't eat out every day. If you want me here, that can't happen all of the time."

"Wow, I didn't know you were going to come over here and start changing everything," I say it as a joke but I think she takes it seriously. She closes the fridge door and gets her shoes.

"I'll bring your shirt to the next practice. Have fun with your clogged artery." I jump up and run to her purse, snatching it up before she can get it.

Stepping between her and the front door."What? Are you going to walk home in the middle of the night?"

"I would rather get taken by a mafia don than stay with you," she huffs. She what?

"Look, I'm sorry. I really didn't mean it. It was just a joke. I never really cared to cook but if you are here, I will buy every cookbook out there and stock my fridge to the max." I let out a nervous laugh.

"Really?" she questions as her eyebrows pull together.

"Yeah, I mean, of course. I really like having you around. Hopefully, it isn't just me but I have strong feelings for you. I know it's crazy to say because we just started being around each other, but we fit together. I want you to stay, please." I put it all out there.

"No," she says simply and shakes her head. My heart drops and I am about to tell her that I will take her home but then she says, "You aren't the only one that feels that way. We can get take-out tonight but that's it. Do you need help picking out food for your house?" She's so serious and it makes me smile. She's staying, she wants this. I could go shopping by myself but I want to spend every day with her. So, I'll use it as an excuse.

"I probably will need some direction. If I go by myself, I will get a bunch of chicken nuggets and hot pockets." That's pretty much all I buy. If I can't microwave it, I don't get it. I don't know what look she's giving me but I feel like a kid being scolded.

"You can have those too but what about real meat? Maybe some fruit and veggies?" Now she's just mothering me.

"I have real meat right here that I can give you." I grab my junk and wink at her. She just shakes her head. "I will need an adult to help me shop."

"Oh, do you know one? I had some questions for them," she laughs.

"I fucking love that sound. That laugh, it's beautiful. You're beautiful." Her cheeks turn a peony pink and her teeth sink into her bottom lip. I cup her face and pull her in for a kiss. It wasn't heated or hungry. It was more intimate than anything we have done. "Come on my little smartass, let's go get some food." I kiss her forehead, put my shoes on, and grab my wallet and keys.

Monday morning I find myself humming while walking to Ash's Coffee House. After getting food Saturday, we stayed in bed talking. I took a picture of us and it is now the wallpaper on my phone. She took what felt like a million pictures. I'm not complaining because I love it but at that point, I was falling asleep. I'm not as young as I once was, sleep is one of my closest friends. I can't stay awake all night, especially after being inside her, on and off for hours. I did talk her into sending me all of them. When I dropped her off she wanted to keep my shirt, I wasn't going to allow her to give it back anyways.

I walk in and the smell of coffee beans invades my senses. The normal crowd is here and some of them are a little aggressive. I hear a guy yelling and I move to see what's going on. Some piece of shit, 25-year-old-looking boy is yelling at the cashier. The same girl that is always behind the counter. Her bright green eyes are glassy and about to spill over. What the fuck? I push my way through the crowd and go behind the counter.

"Hey, Clara. How about you go get something from the back, I got this," I tell her with a soft tone. She nods and runs through the back door.

The guy stares at me and huffs out, "Good, that bitch can't get a simple order made. I want a caramel frappe with whip cream and extra caramel." I smile and nod my head. I don't know what the fuck he just ordered but all I heard was that he wants a pussy drink because his balls haven't dropped yet. I turn around to get a cup and fill it with ice and water. I turn back to him and hold the cup over his head. A second later, I turn it over. He's having a little fit while the cold ice water drips off of his hair and face.

"Get the fuck out of here and keep yourself safe. You never know what's around the corner," I say with a wink. He storms out and everybody starts clapping. I walk to the back to check on Clara and get a mop. After I clean the water up, she tells me that Ash was running late taking Silas to school. That's okay because I'm irritated now anyways. I walk the rest of the way to the gym in a mood. I can't stand people like that. They think because they are bigger, they have the upper hand and can treat people however they want. Such a fucking jackass. I'm going to have to get in a quick workout to release some steam before Ms. Beth gets there. There's no telling what she would say about my reaction. I walk into the gym to a very happy Izzy. She is bouncing on her toes.

"What the hell is wrong with you?" I ask, confused. She is not usually cheery in the mornings.

"I had sex," she practically yells. I can't help but smile.

"Where did you meet her?" I ask even though she was probably drunk and doesn't even remember. She rolled her eyes.

"That isn't the point," she tells me as she walks away. She's worse than any man I know. I follow her to the front counter and I lean over it to get some details. I don't particularly care about them but she has nobody else to share it with. She starts looking up memberships so that she can send out notices.

I smile a little when I ask her about what happened. She doesn't stop what she's doing when she replies with, "Ok, well I don't remember all of that night. I do remember that she tasted like a full-on meal," I laughed so hard at that.

# Chapter 7

# Ash

After hearing what Jace did for Clara, I wanted to show him my appreciation by bringing him a coffee. And maybe I just wanted to see him. I know I'll see him this evening for Silas's soccer practice but I really like being around him, especially after the shitty morning I've had. First, I overslept which made Silas late for school. Since he was late, I had to go into the building to sign him in. Then on my way to the coffee house, I run over something and get a flat tire. Luckily I'm not a fucking damsel and I know how to take care of my own shit. I still need to go buy a new tire because I can't keep driving on a spare. But first, I want to reward my man. I find a spot to park and head to the gym doors.

Before I open the glass door, I see Jace laughing with a beautiful blonde behind the counter. He's leaning over it and holding her wrists. She's smiling big. I can see her perfect dimples and her perfect teeth. I knew it was too good to be true. They aren't just talking either, they are really into whatever's going on between them. This is what I get for trusting another man. I guess I'm always the one that's just not enough. Whatever, he still stood up for Clara so I'm going to tell him thank you. But after that, I am done with men. Done. I push through the door and walk up to him like nothing is wrong. I'm not one to make a scene over a guy. He can't stop talking to her for two seconds to look up and see me. I put the coffee on the counter and say,

"Thank you for helping Clara." I turn around to leave.

"Hey, Ash! Wait up!" He yells after me. I ignore him like the childish person I am and go to my car. I hear his shoes hit the gravel behind me like he's running. He calls again, "Ash!" I get to my car and unlock the door. Just as I'm about to get in, he takes my wrist and spins me around.

"What?!" I yell at him, even though he is right in front of me. I can't believe he is actually going to play stupid.

"What happened?" He asks with concern on his face.

"Nothing, go back to your little princess in there." I spit and roll my eyes. He has the audacity to smile at me. Seriously?

"Are you jealous?" He asks but I don't answer. I'm already fucking tired of this. I just want to go home and eat some ice cream while watching Ross and Rachel argue over their 'break'. Fuck, Silas has practice tonight. Maybe I could just drop him off. He interrupts my thoughts when he starts talking again.

"That's my co-worker," he continues to smile.

"Great," I say, shifting from one foot to the other.

"She was telling me about how she had a great night with somebody," he says.

"Perfect," I give another clipped one-word response.

"Yeah, she seems to be really into the girl that she slept with." Wait, what? He must notice that it all just hit me. He continues, "Yeah, she's a lesbian. And even if she wasn't, I already have the person that I want. Why would I ruin that?" I feel my eyes start to tear up. I let one escape as I try to apologize.

"I am so sorry. I can't believe I let my mind go there. I know better, I'm just so used to being treated like shit. But that's not an excuse. I feel so stupid." At this point, I taste the saltiness of my tears but I make them stop spilling over. He takes me in his arms and holds me tight.

"It's okay, I get it. I understand what it looked like but you have to trust me. That's the only way this will work." He soothes me. I can feel his shirt getting wet so I stand straight and take a look at the spots that I created. I start apologizing for that too.

"Jeez, I'm such a mess. I got your shirt wet. I'm really sorry. Did you bring another one? I can go to the store and get you one. I'll be right back," he starts laughing but doesn't let me go. "Why are you laughing at me?"

He smiles at me for a minute before answering.

"You're just adorable and I love every bit of it." I smile up at him but I still feel stupid. "How about we go back in there and you can meet her." There's no way I can go back in.

I pleaded with him. "I can't face her, she probably thinks I'm crazy. I looked like a jealous girlfriend. She won't like me. Please don't make me do it." He pokes his bottom lip out, he's mocking me.

"She's going to love you," he says, dragging me to the entrance. We walk through the glass doors and I try to stand up straight. Just pretend like nothing happened. Right, Ash. She definitely didn't notice your little temper tantrum. Jace introduces us.

"Ash, this is my friend Izzy. Izzy, this is my girlfriend Ash." She looks me up and down. I just stand there feeling awkward as hell.

"I can see his fascination, he talks about you all the time. I'm happy that I finally get to meet you. Also, I'm not into him," Izzy says. I feel the heat rise to my face.

Embarrassed, I say, "I'm usually not like that. I don't know what happened. It's just that you are very pretty and I have a bad past with men." Now I'm just rambling. She smiles and stops me.

"It's okay, I get it. He's a good guy and all but if he isn't doing it right, just walk my way. I'll take care of you." She winks at me and I can't help but smile. Jace gets between us and interrupts.

"Hey, hey now. Don't try to take my girlfriend from me. I just got my hands on her." He holds me close to him and places a gentle kiss on the top of my head. He's so sweet but I'm not one to be mushy in public. I back away from him and joke around.

"Actually Izzy's idea sounds much better. I think I'll see what she's working with. I'm sure she can find all the spots." His face drops and I start to laugh. "This has been fun but I have to get back to work. Clara is probably losing her mind by now." I give Jace a kiss and walk out. Once I'm in my car, my phone dings with a text message.

> **ASSHAT: You are joking, right? If you leave me for a girl, I won't survive.**

> **ME: Haha. Play your cards right and I won't have to. **winky face****

> **ASSHAT: I will spend extra time on my knees later.**

> **ME: How would you be able to do anything on your knees?**

> **ASSHAT: Just wait, you'll find out.**

> **ASSHAT: Are you bringing Silas to practice?**

> **ME: Yes. The only time that I won't take him is the weekends that his dad has him.**

> **ASSHAT: Does he know about us?**

> **ME: Yes, I had to tell him because you are around Silas.**
>
> **ME: Are you worried about something?**
>
> **ASSHAT: Not at all. I just want to make sure he knows what I will be rubbing in his face.**
>
> **ME: Haha, you have issues.**
>
> **ASSHAT: You have no idea.**

I toss my phone onto the passenger seat and head back to check on Clara. When I get there she is wiping down the counters and there are only a handful of people here drinking their coffees.

"Hey, how did the rest of the morning go?" I ask Clara.

"That guy actually made my day. It all went smoothly after he left," She responds.

"Good. Don't let anybody treat you poorly. Unlike what every other business believes, the customers are not always right. Never allow yourself to get run over. You are an amazing, hardworking woman and you deserve to be treated as such. I will even allow you to say some nasty words to them. Keep your head high," I tell her and then turn to walk away but she calls me.

"So, umm, do you think he's single?"

"Who?" I ask curiously.

"The guy that stood up for me. He is awfully cute," she tells me with the biggest smile. I hate to burst her bubble but...

"He's actually my boyfriend." Her face goes firetruck red and she starts apologizing.

"Oh wow. I'm so sorry. I didn't mean to ogle over your man like that." I can't help but laugh. She is so innocent and adorable.

"Don't be sorry. He is cute and you can stare at him anytime you want. Just keep your hands to yourself or you might lose them." Her eyes got ten times bigger on that last part. I want to tell her that I was just joking but I might actually be serious. Jace brings the crazy out in me. I smile and walk to the back to look into what it will take to upgrade the place.

The week passed by pretty quickly. I ordered the new seating for the coffee house and spent as much time with Jace as I could. Silas had fun having a male figure in his life. Yeah, he has his dad but that is only every other weekend. Jace has been including Silas in almost everything. He has picked him up from school, helped with his homework and I swear I overheard them talking about a new girl in my son's life. I feel incredibly lucky.

He hasn't stayed the night yet because I didn't want to make Silas uncomfortable but I think it's about time. I just need to sit down with him and see how he feels about everything. I am very happy but my son's happiness is important too. It's Friday afternoon and I'm dropping Silas off at his practice, his dad is supposed to be here because it's his weekend. I look around and finally spot him. Fuck, he's talking to Jace. I speed walk over to them. Layne says he doesn't care but who knows, he might start feeling like he needs to be a bitch. It feels like it takes forever but I make it over to them and interrupt their conversation.

"Hey. What's going on?"

"Just asking Coach here about some plays," Layne says. I look over to Jace and he's staring at him with a blank face. I want to push but I don't want Jace getting physical.

"Silas is over there, how about you go talk to him?" I try to get some space to talk to Jace.

"Hey, are you okay? What did he say?" I ask him. He gives me this nonchalant look.

"Nothing I can't handle," he says with a smile. Damnit, Layne better not be fucking this up for me.

"I know you can handle anything but I would like to be nosey. What happened?" I push for an answer. With a kiss on my forehead, he says, "It's fine, really. Stop worrying. Go home and work on that smartass mouth for me. You've been slacking." He gives me a wink.

"Well, it seems you are living up to your asshat title," I retort. "Fine, I'll go home. I need to have some alone time with my vibrator anyways." He's just about to say something when another mom comes up to ask him questions about tomorrow's game. I smirk and go to tell Silas that I'm leaving and I'll see him at his game. Layne has to step in and try to get me mad.

"I'm going to bring Chloe tomorrow," he tries me.

"Go for it. Could you just make sure she doesn't show up with her fake tits hanging out? Also, I know she likes to spray tan, but let her know that the team color is yellow, not orange," I say with the fakest smile that I could muster up. I really don't give a shit about them but I still have that small irritation that just won't go away. I walk to my car and slow my breathing. Before I speed off, I make sure no kids are around. I might not like other people's children, but I don't want to run them over. Well, most of the time I don't want to run them over. I zone out the whole drive to my house. When I get inside, I check my phone. One new message.

> **ASSHAT: You better not cum without me. Every one of your orgasms is mine.**

Oh, this is going to be fun. I get to my bed and strip off all of my clothes. Pull out my favorite Rabbit vibrator and set my phone up to record. Just to add a little more tease to it, I throw in praise.

"Be a good boy and I'll let you taste it later." I lay down on my back and run my fingers through my hair. I bend my knees with my feet still on the bed. Closing my eyes and gliding my fingers down my neck to my breasts. I pinch and pull on my nipples, teasing them. The bar of my piercings makes it a little bit easier to twist and turn them. Picturing Jace's hands on me instead. Moving his hands down my stomach, but instead of going to that sweet spot, He grabs onto my thighs and squeezes. Trailing his hands up my legs, using his fingers to feel the wetness between my folds. I tip my head back when his fingers dip inside my warmth. I give a quiet hum.

Pulling my fingers out, I stick them in my mouth and suck my juices off while I look over at my phone. I smile and grab my Rabbit. I trail it down from my tongue, over my breasts, and make my way down to my slick pussy. I click the magic button and it comes to life. I circle it around my entrance and then push it in. The vibrations hit that spot that has me losing control. The shorter piece, *what I call the clit master*, is also vibrating on my bud. My breathing gets heavier and raspier. I imagine Jace's fingers inside of me and his tongue lapping me up. It's all so much that I can't make it last any longer. My legs start to shake and I moan nice and loud.

"Fuck, Jace. Right there. Yes, yes, yes!"

I lay there for a moment to compose myself. Satisfied, I crawl to my phone.

"I'll be waiting for you to clean me up." I smile and turn the video off. I watch it back to make sure I looked and sounded good. Happy with it, I send it to him. Making sure that I click on his name and nobody else's. I have made the mistake of sending nudes to the wrong person before. It was beyond awkward. I hop out of bed and throw some pajamas on. There's no way I'm staying naked until he gets here. I hate being naked. And since we decided he is staying at my place this weekend, I might as well get comfortable. After all of that, my throat hurts so I go to my kitchen and put on the kettle.

I love hot tea with a little bit of local honey. Deciding which flavor to pick is almost always hard. Peppermint for mornings or period cramps, chamomile for my sleepless nights, and lemon drop for sore throats. Okay, so maybe it's not that hard to choose. I just get overwhelmed sometimes. While I wait for it to start singing, my phone dings. My face starts to sting with the amount of smiling that I have done tonight.

> **ASSHAT: Your ass is fucking mine when I get there.**

> ME: Ooh, I'm so scared... Not really, but it is cute that you think you are in control. You are more like my dog. Sit, stay... Good boy.

> **ASSHAT:** Just wait. You will be the one that's on all fours.

> **ME:** Talk, talk, talk. So many words.

> **ASSHAT:** Practice is over and you are so fucked.

> **ME:** Yeah, yeah. We will see.

    I catch myself smirking and biting my lip. I have never wanted somebody as often as I want him. He brings out the dirty side of me and I'm not mad about it. I toss my phone on my bed. Sliding my tongue over my teeth, I feel a little bit of grittiness. Yuck. Guess I should go fix that and freshen up some. The soccer field is right down the road so now I'm trying to hurry. He is going to be here any minute now. I rush through my teeth and take a brush to my hair.

    Looking in the mirror, I feel like I'm missing something. I look a little dull. A swipe of eyeliner and a small amount of mascara puts it all together. There's a knock at the door and my heart leaps but drops at the same time. I'm excited but stupid nervous. I pretend to be this badass but really, I use sarcasm because I'm scared. I'm scared I won't be enough. I swallow that down and go to the door. Taking one deep breath, I crack the door open. Goddamn. He looks too damn good to have just coached a soccer practice. Black gym shorts, a thin white shirt, and cleats. Wait, what? Who drives in cleats? He pushes the door open more.

"I'm about to put my dick so far inside of you that you are going to feel me hitting your ovaries," he threatens.

"Umm sir, you aren't going to do shit with those cleats on. They are not allowed on my floor," I snap.

"I didn't have time to change my shoes back. There was a video replaying in my head and I had to come to see it first hand," he says while he takes them off. Once they are both off, he reaches around, grabs my ass in both hands and lifts me up on him. I wrap my legs around his hips and kiss him deeply. Kicking the door closed and he starts to walk but I stop him.

"You might keep your door unlocked but I don't want my ex coming by and walking in," I tell him while I turn the lock.

"He stops by?" Jace asked before putting me down.

"Not often but he does sometimes," he looks annoyed.

"I don't share, Ash..." he says irritably.

"He doesn't come to see me. He comes for Silas. You know, his kid? That will never change and he's a good father. Shitty partner but he is good to his son," I explain. This is not going the way it was planned. Trying to get back to where we were, I push his chest hard enough that he has to take a step back.

He looks at me sternly and says, "I get that but I just want to make it clear that you are my girlfriend, and nobody else is allowed to touch or flirt with you. You. Are. Mine. Do you understand?"

I smile because damn, that was hot. I leap up on him and wrap my legs around his hips while he holds onto my ass again. "Ditto." Then I slam my lips on his. His tongue pushes through and I let him in. We battle for dominance. I'm turned on by the fact that he doesn't bow down to me and he actually tries for control. I like the feeling of being wanted, being craved. He walks me into the wall hard enough to feel the bite of pain, but I like it. It makes me wetter, which I didn't think was possible. I grab his shirt and start pulling, I need to feel the heat of his body. He moves to where I can pull it up and over his head, breaking the kiss for only a second. Once it's off, I throw it down, and our mouths meet again. I want my skin on his, I break our kiss again and he groans. He gives me a sexy grin when he sees what I'm doing. As soon as my shirt is off, his teeth find my nipples. He uses his tongue to turn my nipple rings and I moan while I grab onto his hair.

"You changed them," he states. The bars I put in this time have little diamonds on the ends instead of plain balls.

"Yeah, I like to change up so that I don't get boring," I say breathlessly.

"I promise you are anything but boring. Where's your bed? I want to show you just how exciting you really are," he starts nipping at my neck. I crook my head to the side to give him better access.

"My house isn't that big, use your big brain to figure it out." I smile. He comes up from my neck to my ear and whispers.

"Okay smartass, I guess it will take even longer for you to feel how big my other brain is." Nope, I can't do that especially since I know what's in his pants.

"Down the hall on the left," I breathe. I need him inside of me now. With my hands still in his hair, I hook my fingers in it and tug, making him look at the ceiling. I start from the bottom of his neck and lick up until I get to his jaw. Once my tongue feels the roughness of his five o'clock shadow, I stop and lightly bite. I love this on him, I need to make sure I tell him to keep it.

He hums, "Keep doing that and we won't make it to the room." I back off just enough to look into his eyes.

"Well then take me to bed," I say purring and he quickly walks to my room. He drops me on the bed and wastes no time taking mine and his pants off. He closes his eyes and sucks his bottom lip in his mouth.

"You aren't wearing panties again," He lowers his voice to a deep husky tone. He opens his eyes slowly, drinking me in.

"I haven't worn them in a couple of weeks now. I feel they get in the way," I tell him and then he's on me. Kissing me everywhere. He puts his face between my legs but I stop him.

"No, I want to feel you inside of me," I pant. He slaps my outer thigh and I jump.

"Don't ever deny me the opportunity to taste you. I am going to lick you up like ice cream on a fucking hot as-hell day. And you are going to like it. After you cum, I'm going to stick my tongue in that tight little pussy and draw out what I've earned. I want you to be on my tongue for the rest of my life. Now lay back and let me enjoy myself," his voice sounds just like honey to my ears and I could cum just from that. I can't believe he actually likes to be down there. I have never had anybody love to give me oral like this. His tongue swipes up one time and then he blows, making the wetness cold. A good cold. It gives me shivers but I want more. He gently bites my clit. Holy mother of fuck!

"Ah, oh my god! Yes, do that," I breathe. Normally I would be embarrassed but I am so close. He does it again and then he buries his face in me. His hands go under my ass and he lifts. In this position, he can sit on his knees and grab my thighs to keep me up. It's not very comfortable with my ass all the way up in the air and I'm basically just laying on the back of my shoulders. I don't say anything because fuck, it feels good. It doesn't take long and I feel it building, building, building and that's it. I release all over his mouth.

"Jace…" I moan. I start shaking uncontrollably and my legs squeeze his head. When I come back down to earth, he sticks to his word. He looks into my eyes and pushes his tongue in me. His tongue comes out and goes back in. When he is satisfied, he licks me one more time. I am dropped back down on the bed and smile up at him. He gets a condom out of his pants and tears the packet open with his teeth. Blows a piece of the foil out of his mouth and rolls the condom on. I bite my lip so that I don't start drooling. Everything this man does is sexy.

"I'm so lucky," it slips out before I can stop myself. He smiles, lines himself up with my entrance, and slips into me. His head drops to my shoulder and we stay there for a couple of seconds.

"No ma'am, I am the lucky one. The way your pussy tightens around my dick, I can't even dream this up. Shit," he whispers in my ear and then kisses the spot that makes my eyes roll back. The one that's just below my ear. My legs wrap around his waist.

"I need you to move," I beg.

"Maybe I just want to make you suffer for that little stunt you pulled earlier," he teases.

"You're such an asshat, I've learned my lesson. Never deny you. Now fuck me!" I yell at him. And that's all it takes to get him to pull out just a little and push back in. He starts out slow but then his thrust starts to speed up.

"Harder," I tell him. He slams into me but it's still not enough.

"Harder!" I try again. He sits up and turns me around, facing the mattress.

"I told you earlier that you would be the one on your hands and knees," he says. Ugh, how did I let this be turned on me? I didn't get a chance to really think about it because he's pushing himself into me again. When he gets balls deep, I feel his hand slap my ass. Hard. I wiggle my butt to encourage more. He slaps the other cheek. Then his hands grab onto my hips and pulls me back while he pushes forward. He finds a rhythm and he doesn't let up.

"Fuck yes!" I scream. This is what I wanted. What I needed. The sweetness is building again. Before Jace, I had never came more than once. He slaps my ass and I explode on him again. He flips me back over so I'm laying on my back.

He leans down to whisper in my ear, "Now, where is that vibrator?"

"Oh, no no no. I can't cum again." I freak out. He pulls out of me and goes to my bedside table.

"Let's see what's in drawer number one," he says and then opens my top drawer. I only keep condoms, notepads, and pens in there. Once he realizes that, he moves down. I have multiple in there, he's about to find a whole nother side of me. I also have some other questionable tools. "Then it must be behind drawer number..." He loses his words when he pulls it open. "Oh wow." The embarrassment hits and I grab my sheets to cover myself. "What are you doing?" He pulls the sheet off of me and goes back to the drawer. "I'm going to have fun with this. I think I'm going to stick with the vibrator this time but it's nice to know that I can do other things to you." He holds up the handcuffs in one hand and a flogger in the other. "Ash, these aren't furry cuffs," he says.

"It's insane but I can actually see with my eyes. They aren't here just to be pretty." I toss some sarcasm to cover my nerves but he's still waiting for an answer. "Fine, I like the bite. The pain is pleasurable to me." I cover my eyes because, at this point, I know my face is red. He takes hold of my hands in his and kisses them.

"I love that you are open to things. Don't ever be embarrassed around me. There are things that I like too that haven't come to light yet. I mean, you already know that I like your hand around my neck. So don't be shy. At a later time, you are going to have to tell me everything that you want. But for now, I'm going to show you what happens when you tease me over the phone," he says caring, getting me excited for our future. I look down and notice that he is still wearing a condom and somehow, he's still hard. So much has happened and he's still ready for me. That's crazy. He holds my vibrator in front of my face.

"Lick it." He orders. Gaining a little bit more confidence, I make it as slutty as I can. I turn my head to the side, close my eyes and work my tongue from where his hand is to the tip and I circle around it. I take it in my mouth and make a groaning noise. He pulls it out of my mouth and pushes me down on the bed. "How do you feel about being tied up?" He asks.

"I say, you better make the knots tight. But you also have to go buy some rope because all I have are handcuffs," I respond and his face glows. He pulls them out and tells me to scoot up to the head of the bed. I do as he says and he cuffs one wrist, wraps the chain around the metal frame, and cuffs the other. I love my bed set because, with the framework, there are so many possibilities. It being king-size helps too.

"Since you aren't able to run away now, pick a word if you want me to stop," he demands.

"Is it going to get that serious that I will need a safeword?" My voice cracks and my muscles start to tense.

"I don't think so but I want to make sure you know that you don't have to do anything that you don't want to. Nothing will hurt but it may get a little intense," he responds. Okay, I can do this, and I feel my body start to relax again.

Should I go basic and say 'Red'? No, everybody uses that. It sounds silly but I have to ask, "Do you like pineapples on your pizza?"

He has this disgusted look on his face. "Hell no. Please tell me you're not one of those people."

"It tastes amazing! Okay, my word is 'pineapple' because you don't like them," I say with confidence. He sits between my thighs and spreads my pussy lips apart. He makes a noise of appreciation and dives in. He starts licking me but only enough to get me nice and wet. Then he comes up and holds the vibrator on me. He turns it on and I pull at the cuffs. The vibration and the wetness have me getting chills. I'm getting worked up and right before I get to that soul-searching moment, he takes it off me.

He waits for a minute and puts it back. I'm almost there again and he pulls it off me again.

"What the hell?" I almost yell. He doesn't answer me but backs away and pulls the condom off, throwing it on the floor. My eyes follow his hand to his dick. He starts to stroke it but stops.

He offers me his hand and says, "Spit." I do it and his hand goes back to rubbing up and down on his length. I look back up into his eyes and he is staring at me. He holds my gaze as he starts moving his arm faster.

"That feeling that you have right now, the one where you want to be a part of this but you can't. That's how I felt on the field when you were here, teasing me," he torments. I pull on the cuffs again and press my thighs together. He notices and gets back between my legs. Then he continues pleasuring himself. "I couldn't touch myself earlier, so you can't now." He is driving me crazy. I bite my lip while I watch him work himself. He doesn't take his eyes off me. Seconds later he speeds up the movement and starts grunting. "Damn, Ash. Fuck, you look so good," he moans and cum shoots out onto the top of my pussy. Shit, why did that have to be so hot? "I'm going to go get a washcloth," he tells me.

"No. Leave it. I like the feeling of your juice on me," I purr and bite my bottom lip. He just stands there and stares at me.

After a few seconds, he finally speaks. "That is the sexiest thing I have ever heard. Unlike you, I'm not mean. I won't leave you there horny." He lays on his stomach and starts eating me. With all of the build-up and teasing, I cum quick and hard. He licks up all of it and rises to his knees. He leans over me and grabs the key off of the table and unlocks the cuffs. When my wrists are free, he takes them and kisses all over.

"Thank you for sticking that out. I know how difficult that can be." He gently kisses my forehead. I rub my hand through the sticky cum I made him leave on me. He smiles and gets up, going into my joint bathroom and I hear the shower turn on. Minutes later, he comes back.

"We must be in sync. I was just going to tell you that I need a shower," I laugh. He helps me stand up and I would have fallen if he wasn't holding onto me. My legs are shaky and weak. I guess multiple orgasms can do that to you. He picks me up bridal style and carries me to the shower. He puts me down and showers with me. After we are clean and smelling good, we just stand there, under the running water. My back to his chest. He wraps his arms around me and I hold onto him. My head falls back to his chest and I feel the exhaustion hit me.

It's game night and I am pumped. I love watching Silas get out there and play his heart out. He uses soccer as an outlet. He isn't traumatized or anything and he didn't care about his dad and I splitting. He just has a lot of teenage hormones. I lucked out and made a boy that isn't a dick. He has dickish moments but we all do. I'm wearing a bright yellow t-shirt and jeans with holes in the knees. I used eyeliner to write his number on my cheeks. He's number five. I also bought a damn fold-up chair. Jace told me to sit by the bench but I don't want to stand out. This is about Silas and I'm not taking anything away from him. So I am sitting in line with the other parents.

I do feel awkward because they are blatantly staring at me. We were very obvious after the first game. It's okay though, they can be jealous little bitches. I can't help it if their husbands aren't fucking them right. I sit here with my chin held high and a smile on my face. Fuck them. The game is starting and they are doing the coin toss. It's the other team's ball and they all take their spots on the field. Silas is taking midfield and he was ready to play when we talked earlier. I try to keep up with the terms and rules but there are some things I am still learning. The other team looks like they have their shit together. They are communicating and passing the ball back and forth. Damn, do they practice every fucking day? This is crazy. The Gladiators haven't even touched the ball. Within five minutes of starting, the other team scored a goal. It looks like our goalie is taking it pretty hard. The rest of the team catches an attitude and I can hear them blaming each other. I try to sit here and stay quiet but there's no way that they will play well if they keep this up. Before I can stop myself, I am walking over to Jace. I know I shouldn't but he isn't doing anything about this problem.

"Coach," I yell out. He turns to me and his face is unreadable.

"What's up?" He responds.

"Are you going to fix their attitude? Maybe encourage them a bit?" I say with an attitude of my own.

"And what would you like me to do about it? They are in the middle of a game," he deadpans.

"Call a timeout and talk to them," I tell him as a matter of factly. He looks at me like I'm stupid but then straightens himself up and smiles. He goes back to coaching and I just stand there. Why isn't he calling it? I put my hands on my hips, waiting. I stay put for the rest of the first half. Once the ref calls half-time, Jace walks back to me. He gets close enough that only I can hear him.

"If you're going to be a smartass on my field, make sure you know what you are talking about," he clips and I almost want to bite back but I hold my tongue while he finishes. "There are no timeouts in soccer. Players can be switched when the ball isn't in play but we can not call for it like in football. Now, you can stay here if you are quiet or go sit with the other parents." He's lucky that I already know I'm in the wrong or I would tell him to go fuck himself. I turn and walk back to my chair. On the way there I pass Layne.

"Trouble in paradise?" He asks but doesn't actually care.

"Nope, just a little foreplay for later." I give him a wink. He brought his blow-up doll with him but she isn't stupid enough to step up and say anything. Good for her. Once I get back to my seat, fucking Darla has something to say.

"Did he send you back to your seat? Maybe he needs somebody else that can keep up with things." She says with a smirk.

"Maybe, but you already tried and got rejected on the spot. So go suck a dick, I'm already on his." I snap. Her mouth drops open like she can't believe I said that. I don't care. She can go fuck herself. I guess everybody is fucking themselves today. Fuck them all. I pull some gum out of my pocket, pop it in my mouth and go to town on it. I keep gum on me all the time just in case I get mad enough to hit somebody. I take a few minutes to calm myself down and get back to watching the game.

My baby has the ball and is running but then passes it to his teammate once he crosses the center line. He has to stay back, something about being offsides? I don't know. I should probably start asking questions now that I'm in a serious relationship with a coach. Wait, did I just say serious relationship? Is this serious? I think it is. I wonder if he feels the same way. We should probably have that talk. The rest of the game goes by in a blur. I was too deep in thought. When the ref blows the whistle ending the game, I immediately feel terrible for not paying attention. The best mom award goes to this one right here.

## Chapter 8

## Jace

"We lost. That's okay. We won't win every game and that's life. But what we can do is talk about what happened tonight on that field. So, what happened?" I question the boys. I have them taking a knee on the sideline. I know what happened but I need them to realize, so they won't let it get that far again. Jordan, one of my defense speaks up.

"The other team scored and it got me mad." I really like that answer because I want them to understand their feelings. These guys are going through physical and mental changes and I want to help them figure it out. I don't want them to see me as just their coach, I want them to see me as somebody that cares for them. I want to help them grow, not just as a soccer player.

"I understand that but why let that anger stay with you and take over? We just lost the game because our emotions weren't under control. We can be mad but it needs to be dropped by the time the ball gets in play. The next game will be better because now we know the consequences of holding on to that anger. Yes?"

"Yes, Coach," they say in unison.

"Start strong..." I start.

"Finish strong!" They all finish for me. They can do this. I can see that they want this, they want to learn. I am honored that I get to help them.

"See y'all Monday evening. Get gone." I smile and wave them off. Now onto the next fire. I look around but can't find Ash. I see Silas and dumbass but she isn't there. There's a woman with dumbass. I forgot his name, honestly. I am too nosey to just walk away.

"Hey, Silas," I call as I start to approach them.

"Coach. Thanks for not yelling after the game." He says, timidly looking down.

"Why would I yell?" I tilt my head, taken aback by his statement. I look over and his dad is facing the opposite way. Oh, I get it. Not wanting Silas to get in any trouble, I turn to his dad. I've met him already but not his friend. "Nice to see you again, umm, I'm sorry, what was your name again?" I ask but really, I just want to piss him off. He finally faces me and looks me up and down.

"Layne. This is my girlfriend, Chloe." He introduces. I don't know her story so I can't judge but I'm also not going to start problems with Ash, so I keep my mouth shut.

"Where's your mom?" I ask Silas.

"Oh, she left after the game. I'm going home with my dad so she didn't need to stick around," he answered. We fist bump and I go back to the bench and pull my phone out. I wish these parents would take the boys home, I'm ready to leave. I check my phone but there are no messages. Damnit. I didn't do anything wrong and if she wants to continue this relationship, she has to know that she can't do shit like that again. I send her a text.

> **ME: Am I still allowed over?**

I stand there waiting for what feels like a lifetime. She always has her phone on her. Is she ignoring me? I hate it when girls do that shit. I would much rather you tell me to fuck off than be ignored. My phone dings in my hand. Finally.

> **MY SMARTASS: Yeah, we need to talk anyway.**

Are you fucking kidding me? Why do people do that? That is the worst text anybody could get. I run to my car and hop in. Put my seatbelt on, throw this bitch in drive, and head to her house. It doesn't take long before I am pulling up in her driveway. I rush to the door and start banging on it. Not knocking, but about to tear the door down banging. She swings the door open and she looks irritated.

"What the hell is wrong with you?" She interrogates.

"Me?" Am I going crazy? "Me? What's wrong with me?" I ask with a little irritation.

"Yeah. You are hammering on my door like there are fucking zombies and you need to get in." Of course, she responds with some off-of-the-wall shit.

"You said that we needed to talk," I say, cutting all the shit and getting straight to it. She walks into her house and comes back with her keys.

"Let's take a walk." Another scary statement. I step aside and let her lead the way. We walk a good mile before I can't take it anymore.

"Are you ending this?" I ask, holding my breath. She scrunches her eyebrows together like she's confused.

"No! I just wanted to talk about where we stood with each other!" She exclaims. I was about to push further but I look around and come to a stop. We are walking down a path where there's a long line of shops on both sides. Above us are string lights running across from one shop to the other side of the path. It's beautiful and I can't believe that I didn't know about this place.

"Wow, this is breathtaking. Has this been around for a while?" I ask her.

"I think about eight or nine years. I like coming out here at night. I wanted to show you my favorite place to go when I need a break from life. It calms me." She admits.

"Thank you for sharing this with me. I love it." I bite my tongue after I let that last bit out. I've wanted to tell her what I feel for her for the past week but I was too nervous that it was too soon and she would run. But I got to tell her, it's eating at me. I reach out and hold her hand.

"I love you, Ash," I confess. She looks me in the eyes and holds me there. I feel my palms getting sweaty. But then she smiles and leaps in my arms and starts kissing me, in front of everybody. I am still waiting for her to respond because I need to hear the words if she feels the same. She breaks the kiss and I set her back down.

"Jace, I brought you out here to tell you that I love you!" She blurts with a big ass smile. My world stood still in that moment. I wrapped my arms around her waist and lifted her off of her feet and kissed her. I put her down and started talking while still on her lips.

"We are going to go back to the house so that I can show you how much I love you." She grabs onto my hair and pulls me deeper into the kiss. Her tongue is on my lips begging for me to let it in. I open my mouth slightly and give in to her.

"Hey! There are children out here!" Some guy yells out. We start giggling and she pulls her phone out wanting a picture. I will give her as many pictures as she wants as long as it keeps that beautiful smile on her face. I tell her to send them to me and we walk hand and hand back to her house. I don't remember the last time that I was this happy. When we make it back, we walk to her bedroom and slowly start taking our clothes off. We aren't in any kind of rush. We get in bed and make love all night. I had to take a break in between because food was needed and I'm not a fucking porn star, my dick doesn't stay hard after cuming. Most people would say the sex we had was boring and slow but for me, it was the best I've ever had because it was love. It wasn't just fucking to get off. It's cheesy as hell but it was like we shared our souls.

We finally fell asleep after what I think was hours. I left my phone in my car so I have no idea. I was going to get it but there's nobody worth talking to and taking time away from her. I'm so fucking in love with this woman that I'm not scared to take the leap. I wake up with her curled up on my chest and I can't be any happier. I want this every morning. Would it be crazy to ask her to move in? I probably shouldn't because it might be too much for Silas. Am I ready to take on the responsibility of a kid? Hell no, but I don't think anybody is ever ready. I've spent some time with him off the field and he seems like a good kid but at the same time, he's a teenager. One word...hormones. Yeah, that's going to be a ride. I don't want to move and wake her but I'm about to piss on myself. I try to slowly and easily slide from under her but I fail. She stirs and smiles.

"Good morning, princess," she rolls over and says with a sleep-filled voice.

"I think you must have forgotten who you fell asleep with. I am not worthy of such a title." I say back to her and she giggles. "Good morning, smartass." I kiss her forehead and basically jump out of bed and run to the toilet. I finish my business, wash my hands and hop back in bed.

"My nickname is so sweet. How could a woman not fall for you?" She nitpicks.

"Well, you started off as a smartass and you keep proving the name fitting," I reply.

"That's okay because your name is asshat in my phone." She smiles.

"Now who is the sweetest? At least your name is MY smartass in mine," I joke with her.

"Awe, that's so romantic," She croons and leans over for a kiss. But then she stops before she gets close and runs to the bathroom. She probably has to pee too. I sit here for a minute and I hear the sink running. I get up to see what she's doing. She's putting toothpaste on her toothbrush. I rush over to her and snatch it out of her hand and put it on the counter. I turn her around and trap her between my arms and the counter.

"Stop, my breath is so bad when I wake up," she cries out. I lean in and capture her lips with mine. She wasn't lying, it is bad.

"I'm not here just for the good, I want the bad too. I want all of it. But I'm going to go get my phone and let you brush your teeth. It is pretty fucking bad," I joke with her. She slaps me on my shoulder and has this embarrassed smile. I leave her to do her business and grab my keys. Getting my phone, I head back inside and check it. Surprisingly it still has some battery left. No missed calls and no text messages. That's the beauty of being antisocial. I lay my phone down on the counter when Ash walks into the living room.

"What do you want me to cook you for breakfast?" I ask her. She starts laughing and tries to compose herself.

"There's no way in hell you are cooking anything. I would like to live another day." She continues to laugh.

I'm glad she knows because all I could whip up for her are eggs. And they won't even be fluffy. She goes to the kitchen and starts making pancakes.

"Do you have chocolate chips?" I inquire. She just stares at me for a moment.

"Umm, yeah. My fifteen-year-old likes it that way. Which reminds me, how old are you?" She catches me off guard but I guess we haven't actually talked about that.

"Thirty-five," I simply say. Her eyes widen and she goes back to cooking. That look almost has me scared so I walk up behind her, wrap my arms around her and put my face in the crook of her neck. "What was that?" I ask nervously.

"You are just so old," She says with lightness in her voice. That soothes my fear a bit.

"There's no way that I'm that much older than you," I say and nip her neck. She squirms and lets out a sigh.

"Sir, I am only thirty. So it's like dating somebody's dad." She takes me by surprise.

"Oh yeah, do you want me to be Daddy?" I ask and then lick her neck. She starts giggling.

"Oh no, sorry but I am not into that. But I'm sure we can figure something out." She states as she's stacking pancakes on a plate. She goes to get a cup and I take it out of her hand.

"I know for a fact that I can pour a drink. It's one of my specialties." I preen with a wink. That makes her smile and she shakes her head. I make two cups of orange juice and set them down on the table. She already brought the plates of pancakes, syrup, and forks. I sit and start to eat but decide I want to make a show of it.

"Oh wow, this is so good. It's like my mouth just had the best orgasm," I moan. "It's like when I eat you and you cum. Licking up every little bit of that sweetness." I was just playing around but my dick got hard, fast. She stares at me with her mouth open. Good, I'm getting to her. What I don't expect is when she pulls her shirt off, grabs the syrup, and squeezes it out on her nice, perky breasts. My plan turned on me. She puts the bottle down and wipes her middle finger in it and spreads it over her nipple. Then she puts her finger in her mouth and sucks it off. That is the hottest thing I've ever seen. Shit. I can't sit here anymore, I'm on her so fast. I pick her up and sit her on the table.

The syrup has trailed down to her pajama shorts. I gently push her back to lie down, pull her shorts off, and of course, she's not wearing panties. This woman is going to kill me. I lick the sticky brown sugar off of her stomach and trail my way up to her nipple. Licking and sucking, getting it all off. It's all gone but I stay there and play with it some more. Her breathing is heavy and I can feel her heart pumping faster than normal. I stand up and grab the bottle, pour a little bit on her thighs then set it down and get on my knees. I start licking and nibbling up her leg, keeping my eyes on her face. She bites her lip and looks down at me.

"You look so good on your knees for me," she breathes out. I grab her thighs and try not to squeeze too hard. She seems to like that because her toes curl and I make my way to her throbbing pussy. I don't start out slow, I dive right in. Licking, sucking, and lightly biting. She moans and her back arches off the table.

"Shit. Ahh. Yes, yes, yes. Jace! I'm going to cum!" She screams out. Her legs started shaking and her hands find my hair. She pushes my face into her more and I breathe her in. Fuck, I can't get enough of this. She rides her orgasm out and I lick it all up. I stand back up and lick my lips while I rub my dick through my pants. She slides off of the table and walks away. A second later, she comes back with a can of sprayed whipped cream. When she gets to me, she drops to her knees. Puts the can on the floor and yanks my shorts and briefs down. "I'm not a fan of that much syrup and you have a lot of surface to cover." She winks looking up at me. She sprays a line of it on my length and licks it off while keeping eye contact. This is a picture that I won't be letting slip from my brain any time soon. Her puffy pink lips wrap around me and it doesn't take long at all before I am warning her.

"Ash, I'm about to cum." She takes me out of her mouth with a pop.

"Cum for me. All the way down my throat," She says and puts me back between her lips. That's all it takes and I'm coming undone. I try not to but I close my eyes and tip my head back. My hands go behind my head so that I don't push her too far. When I come down from the high, I watch her swallow and it's so fucking hot. She licks the tip to get everything. *I'm going to marry her one day.*

I help her to her feet and we kiss. I taste myself on her tongue but I don't even care.

"Move in with me," I blurt out before I can stop myself.

"Aren't we moving really fast?" She asks.

"Yes, but why deny something that is there? We love each other. I can't speak for you but I want to come home to you every night and sleep beside you." I admit.

"Tell me the story of your huge house," she demands. Well shit, here we go.

"I bought it for me and my ex. I thought we were in love and I was planning on having a family with her. But it didn't happen and I am so happy that it didn't because I love what we have," I tell her and hold my breath.

"Look, we all have a past, I don't care about that. I had a kid with somebody, so how could I hold you wanting a family against you? I'm pretty down to earth. But I won't be living in that house. I'll be a little petty. Maybe we can take that step one day but not today," she says a lot calmer than I thought she would. I honestly thought that she would be pissed.

"I fucking love you." I chuckle and she smiles up at me.

"I fucking love you too." She giggles and we stand there staring at each other like creeps until she breaks the silence. "I'm sticky and it's bothering me. Shower time."

"Okay, sounds good." I agree and walk around her.

"You know you don't have to shower with me if you don't want to. I just don't want you to feel like you have to," she says.

"Right, because I can get tired of seeing you naked and wet. Get your ass in there," I order. We take a shower and after we finished, we go out to eat because the pancakes were cold and it was now lunchtime.

"So I think we should stay in public for a little while. We can't seem to not be naked around each other. As much as I love it, I kinda want to know more about you. I already know your body very well," she suggests.

"When do we pick Silas up?" I ask.

"Umm, we? No, no, no. I need to talk to Silas about this," she says.

"I thought he was okay with us being together." I worry and take a step back.

"He was okay with us dating. But now I need to tell him how serious we are. My son's opinion means a lot to me, especially when it comes to things involving his life as well. Because he will always be here," She clips with a bit of an attitude.

"Hey, hey now. I knew that from the beginning. I know he is your son and I know he is very important to you, which means he is also very important to me. Please don't ever accuse me of putting Silas on the back burner. This is what I signed up for. Every little bit of it. Your son, your ex and his girlfriend, the owner of a business, and the fucking attitude," I snap at her a little too harshly.

"I'm sorry. I don't know why I even thought it. I know all of that, I think I'm just scared. I'm crazy about you and I don't want to get hurt again," she admits.

"I was cheated on as well, remember that. It's in the back of my mind too but this is worth taking that chance," I remind her.

"It is worth it. I still need to make sure he is okay with how deep we are into this," She says.

"Okay, well what time do I have to give you up?" I ask, already unhappy with any answer.

"He comes back to me at five tonight. But don't worry, you can hang out with him tomorrow afternoon, on the field. Wait, how did you phrase it? Oh right, on YOUR field." She smiles.

"Look, I know we are together and everything but I am the coach. And honestly, you don't know shit about the sport. I'm just glad nobody heard you trying to call a timeout." I can't hold back my laugh. She smacks me on the chest and we go back to her house. When we get there, we lay on the couch and talk. There has been so much sex that I just don't have the energy for anything right now. We talk about the basic stuff like food, music, and movies. I had to bring up all of the smut she reads. Her bookshelf is nothing but books with half-naked men on them.

"I like to live in that world just a little bit. I never actually want that stuff to happen to me but it's fun to imagine it," she explains.

"You mean you don't want a bunch of sex?" I ask, baffled.

"Those books aren't just plain Jane sex. They are mafia lords, serial killers, stalkers, and kidnappers. I don't actually want to be taken and forced to marry a Don. But it's so hot to read about," she says but I think she is out of her mind.

"Be honest with me here. Who hurt you?" I can't think of one reason why somebody would read that.

"You joke but that's how I cope. Plus, those guys sound delicious. The way they will kill anybody that touches their woman. Mmm. I just eat that shit up." She tries her damndest to explain.

"Okay crazy. I hate to tell you this but I won't be killing anybody. I may beat the shit out of them if it needs to happen, but that's as far as it will go." I give her full warning.

"Such a disappointment," she laughs it off. Her phone rings and she answers. After a couple of minutes, she hangs up and tells me she's going to get Silas. That's my cue to pack up and leave. I kiss her at the door, get in my car and drive home.

## Chapter 9

## Ash

"Hey, bud, can I talk to you for a minute," I ask Silas once he finishes washing the dishes.

"Mom, I'm really tired. I just want to go to bed." He lies to me. He just wants to get to his room and stalk this girl online. The one that I still don't know anything about.

"It will only take a minute, I promise. Come sit down, I only asked to sound nice. You don't actually have a choice." I use the Mom card on him. He sits in the chair across from me at the table. The table that I scrubbed because I was getting eaten on it this morning.

"Jace and I are getting pretty serious. I wanted to make sure that you are still okay with this?" I ask nervously.

"What would happen if I didn't like it?" He answers the question with a question and I get scared.

"Well, I would call him right now and end it. Tell him that it's not going to work out and that I'm sorry," I answer him but I don't really like where this is going.

"It's a good thing he's pretty cool. I don't care if you are dating him." He shrugs and I let out the breath I was holding.

"If he is a part of my life, he will be a part of yours too. He will be an important factor. Do you understand that? He will be around a lot and we will possibly all live together one day." I explain to him because he needs to know what he's saying he is okay with.

"I know what a serious relationship is, I'm not stupid. I don't care if Coach is around all the time. But I won't call him dad." He smiles.

"That won't be a problem. I also have no plans to have any more kids. You are the only walking hormone I can handle. Are you positive that you are all good with us going forward with our relationship?" Really hoping he says yes.

"I will be happy no matter what. You can marry him and we can move into his house tomorrow if you want. I. Don't. Care." He deadpans.

"Okay, get out of here and go call her." I wave him off and he jumps out of his chair running to his room. Perfect, I go to my room to get my phone. After that conversation, I realize that I never told Jace I don't want any more kids. Hopefully, that won't be a deal breaker. But that's a conversation to have in person.

> ME: We are good to go.

> **ASSHAT: I was just going to pay him off if he had a problem.**

> **ME: It's scary because I know you would actually do that.**

> **ASSHAT: I mean, I go for what I want and crazy, but I want you.**

> **ME: There's something that I need to talk to you about.**

> **ASSHAT: Nope, fuck that. Last time you said some shit like that, I almost had a heart attack.**

> **ME: Haha, It's not like that at all. But I do want to talk about it face-to-face.**

> **ASSHAT: Or, hear me out, I can just call you and take care of that now.**

I think about it for a minute. Fuck it, the conversation will be the same no matter what. So, I call him. He picks up on the first ring.

**"Hey. So, what's up?"**

"I don't want any more kids." There, I said it. Now I'm going to hold my breath.

**"Okay, that's it?"**

"Well yeah, I thought that maybe you would want some."

**"I was hoping that I could be a role model to Silas. To show him how a real man treats his woman instead of how his dad cheated."**

"That sounds perfect. I just didn't know if you wanted any of your own."

**"I am happy with just having Silas. It's a good thing. I get to skip the diapers and the crying. It's all a plus to me.."**

"I'm so happy you said that. I was so worried you would have an issue with it. I take a birth control pill every night but that isn't always effective. That's why I tell you to wear a condom every time."

**"Why haven't you got your tubes tied if you don't want any more?"**

"It's expensive and not medically needed. Plus, I would use a condom anyway to protect myself from any diseases. I've been single for a while and have had some companions."

**"Okay. I was just wondering. I would love to feel you but I'm okay with wearing a condom."**

"I'm sure I will get it done when and if I get married."

**"Do you want to get married?"**

"Yes, one day I would like to. But no time soon. What about you? Do you see yourself as a married man in the future?"

**"Well, since you said you want to, it looks like I will be."**

"Do you think you are going to stick around that long and get shackled by me?"

"**I am not going anywhere. I can't see myself with anybody else. When I fell for you, I fell hard. I could never leave you or let you walk away. You are mine forever.**"

"How am I supposed to call you an asshat when you say shit like that? Don't get all sappy on me now."

"**It won't happen again. Even when I talk you into marrying me, I will be that asshat that you love so much.**"

"Perfect, I expect nothing less. I love you."

"**I love you too.**"

"I'm going to get cleaned up and go to bed. People want their coffee in the morning."

"**Sweet dreams. I love you.**"

"I love you too. Goodnight."

I end the call and drop it on the bed, then go to check on Silas. He's still on the phone, so I go back to my room and lock my door. Turning on the shower, I undress and before I get in, I have an idea. I run back to my bed and pick up my phone and press the camera button. I go back to the shower and get in, careful not to get my phone wet. I take a picture of the water running down my breasts. Take one of the water going down my ass. I send it to Jace and toss it onto the bath mat. I shave, wash my hair and body before I get out. I dry off and pick my phone back up. Checking it to see if he responded, he doesn't disappoint.

> **ASSHAT:** Damn, Ash. I want to lick the water up. Stop at your nipple and turn the bar with my teeth. Fuck, you have me hard, again.

> **ME:** You can't keep yourself in control?

> **ASSHAT:** Fuck no. Not with your body. Shit, I'm so fucking lucky that it's all mine.

> **ME:** Yours? Why do you think this is yours?

He sends me a picture of him laying on his bed with his dick in his hand. Hard and delicious. He has the phone back far enough that I can see the V right below his six-pack.

> **ASSHAT:** Because this is all yours.

> **ME:** Mmmm, the things that I could do with that.

> **ASSHAT:** As long as you don't bite, I'm here for it.

**ME:** What about sliding my teeth over it?

**ASSHAT:** I would rather have nothing sharp near my favorite body part.

**ME:** I'll just get it wet and make it sloppy.

**ASSHAT:** Such a tease. Let me come to you so that I can cum all over you.

**ME:** I have never swooned so hard.

**ASSHAT:** I have to get this thing down. I have somebody to train tomorrow.

**ME:** I guess you better jump on that then.

**ASSHAT:** I would much rather you jump on it.

> **ME: Having you inside of me is one of my favorite feelings.**
>
> **ASSHAT: I love feeling you wrapped around my dick. So wet and tight. Fuck, Ash.**
>
> **ME: Think about me riding you. Your hands grabbing my breasts. Fingers pinching my nipples and my nails digging into your chest.**
>
> **ME: Be a good boy and cum for me.**

The phone goes silent for a couple of minutes and then he texts back.

> **ASSHAT: Fuck that was good. God, I love you.**
>
> **ME: I love you too. Get some sleep.**

I realize I never did get dressed so I get up and put on a loose shirt and night shorts. I stopped wearing panties altogether now. At first, it was because I wanted to be sexy for Jace but now it's actually pretty comfortable. I go check on Silas one last time and he fell asleep with his lights on. Again. I'm not sure how hard it is to turn the light off when you start to get tired. This boy is killing my light bill. Turning it off, I close his door and get in my bed. Jace has worn me out this weekend. The bed feels too big and cold now. I'm already used to him being here. I'm so pathetic. I make sure my alarm is on and put my phone on the charger. Turn my light off and pass out almost immediately.

Monday morning wasn't as bad as I thought it would be. I got Silas to school on time and I even showed up to work early. The only thing I forgot to do was eat, I always forget that. I'm just hardly ever hungry. I can't complain about that because then people tell me how lucky I am. Just because I'm skinny, doesn't mean I'm healthy. Sometimes when I look in the mirror I just feel sick. I want to have meat on my bones.

"Earth to Ash," Clara says, waving a hand in front of my face.

"Oh, sorry. What did you say?" I ask, a little confused.

"I asked you how your weekend went," she repeats.

"It was heaven. But Silas's team lost their game." I admit.

"Oof, that must be rough for him," she sympathizes.

"Yeah, well he needs to learn how to lose and not cry about it," I snap at her.

"Okay then. I didn't mean to hit a touchy subject. Sorry." She holds her hands up defensively. Damnit, I can't believe I did that.

"No, I'm sorry Clara. I shouldn't have bit your head off like that. I haven't eaten anything this morning and it's catching up to me." I apologize and close the distance between us with a hug. I don't remember the last time I bit her head off like that. Actually, now that I am thinking about it, I don't think we have ever disagreed. It feels wrong. She breaks the hug.

"It's okay. But you should go get some food," she says.

"I will but I want to be here for the first rush when we open," I tell her and look at the time on my phone. "Oh look, that would be now. Are you ready to rock and roll?" I ask her. She starts to giggle.

"Yes, as long as you never say that again." She giggles. She is the sweetest person that I have ever met. I go unlock the door and walk back behind the counter. I throw on my best fake smile and welcome the crazy coffee people who walk in. Some of these people wait at the door for us to open. As I said, they are crazy…bananas. Is it bad that the only way that I can spell bananas is to sing the song by *Gwen Stefani?* I'm a sad human being. The people start spilling inside. It turns into mad chaos within seconds.

"Hey! Single file line! Act like y'all know how to behave! I will close this bitch down!" I yell at them. I can't stand when adults act like small children.

"Well damn, if that isn't the sexiest thing." Jace pops up. I didn't know he was even here. I must have looked crazy.

"Oh, umm, sorry about that. I didn't know you were getting coffee this morning," I say, a little embarrassed. He gets close to me and kisses my cheek.

"I would come to see you even without the coffee. But I won't say no to it." He winks and gives me that sexy smirk.

"Fine, still want it as black as your soul?" I ask with a straight face.

"Nah, that would be too milky. I want it without the sweet creamer," he plays along.

"So you think your creamer is sweet?" I can't help but make everything sexual with him.

"Well I mean, you had no problem licking it up and swallowing it," he quips back. I feel my face heating. Nope, we can not do this at my work. I turn around to the coffee machine and bite my lip. With as many times as I've done that with him, I wouldn't be surprised if I bite a hole right through it. I pour his coffee into one of my personal cups I like to keep around for me. It looks like an elephant. I love it. I hand it to him and he looks at me like he's questioning everything.

"When did you start giving out fancy cups?" He asks.

"That is my cup and I fully expect you to bring it to my house soon," I answer.

"Are you saying that it's okay to be at your house while Silas is there?" He starts bouncing on his toes.

"Yes you can, but nothing sexual. I don't want to kiss or anything like that with him there. He says he's okay and I believe him, but that doesn't mean I have to shove it down his throat." I warn him.

"I totally get it. I will try my best to keep my hands to myself. I will even take him in the backyard and kick the ball around," he says and I feel my eyes start to fill. "Oh, I'm sorry. Did I say something wrong?" He takes a step towards me, reaching a hand out in an attempt to comfort me.

"No, not at all. I just never thought that I would have a man that wanted to spend time with my kid too, not just me. I love it." I admit and wipe my eyes because this is embarrassing.

"Hey, it's okay. Of course, I want to spend time with Silas. He's your son and one day, I hope he can be mine too. Well, stepson, but I will treat him like my own." He reassures me and kisses my forehead. This has to be too good to be true. There's no way that there is this man in my life that checks all of the boxes.

"Alright, no more of this shit. Get out of here and go work on those muscles. You seem to be slacking a bit," I tease him.

"Slacking? Excuse me? I am not slacking, I'll show you how much I am not slacking, a little later." He gives me a wink.

"I look forward to it," I challenge. He leans in and kisses me on the lips this time.

"I love you," he simply says.

"I love you too," I say back. He turns and I watch him leave. I swear, he better not break my cup. I stand there and watch him leave. His ass is perfect in those gray, cotton shorts. His muscles are pushing the white t-shirt's limit at the seam. It looks like it's going to rip apart. I want to rip it apart. Damn, he is sexy.

"Ash, I don't mean to pop your sex bubble but is there any way I can get a hand?" Clara asks, dragging me out of my dream world.

"Oh, I'm sorry. Yes, what do you need?" I ask.

"Can you make the coffee while I take the orders?" she requests.

"Yes ma'am," I say with enthusiasm. I go to the fancy ass machine that does the work. We can make regular coffee, iced coffee, frappe, expresso, and more but we don't usually get anything else. We do offer specialty drinks when the season changes but I don't have anything for the spring. So we stick to the basics. Clara calls out the first order and I get to work. Three hours pass by in a flash. Most orders were iced coffees. But there were people that stuck with the expressos they ordered every morning. *They should probably slow down on them or get some kind of help.*

"Clara, how about take a little break? You definitely earned it," I tell her and she gives the biggest smile. She runs out of the shop so fast that it makes me dizzy. I hope she doesn't go too far. Nobody walks in for the next hour and that gives me a much-needed quiet moment.

I hear the door open and put on my perfected fake smile.

"Welcome to the coffee house." I welcome whoever it is, not turning around. It stays quiet so I look over my shoulder and see Jace. My smile turns real and I show off my imperfect teeth.

"It's lunchtime." He informs me like that should mean something to me right now besides the influx of customers surely headed my way. I notice a bag in one hand and flowers in another.

"I must have lost track of time. I usually just eat crackers," I let him know. He shakes his head and looks down at his feet.

"I will not allow my girlfriend to starve. I brought you a sub. It has bacon, chicken, mushrooms, and a shit load of ranch." He hands over the bag.

"Awe, thank you. This actually sounds really good. Definitely better than plain crackers. Who are the flowers for?" I ask.

"Oh, these? These are for me. I have so many women bending over backward for me and one of them gave me these," he jokes.

"Well, then you better run to your house and put them in water." He puts his nose in the bouquet of orange and white carnations.

"They do smell pretty good. It might be my second favorite smell," he tells me.

"Second? You must tell me first. What is the smell that you have to have? What is the smell that drops you to your knees and makes your mouth water?" I ask him, leaning on the counter. He walks up to me, the counter between us is the only thing that is keeping my hands off of him.

"The smell that I can't live without or I might die…" He almost finishes until some girl walks in.

"How can I help you?" I ask, rushed.

"Can I get a half-caf?" She orders. I rush through the motions of taking her money and making her coffee. I put a sleeve on it and hand it to her.

"Have a great day," I say as she leaves. I walk back over to Jace continuing our conversation.

"Please, finish," I encourage.

"The smell that has my mouth watering is that pretty pink pussy between those thighs I love wrapped around my head," he whispers so close I feel his breath touch my face. That is all it takes and I feel the wetness pooling between my thighs.

"Nope! No, sir! I am not going to do this at work. Take that sexy mouth and shut it!" I order.

"I know a few things that I can do with my mouth. If I use my hands and mouth, that would be a ride," He growls in a seductive voice at my ear.

"Stop it. I don't want to do this at work." I try again, meaning it this time. He puts the flowers down on the counter and holds his hands up in surrender.

"Okay, I will hold onto all of this built-up energy," he states finally and takes a step back.

"How did you know that carnations are my favorite?" I question. I am actually inquisitive.

"I asked Silas. He actually knows you pretty well. Most kids his age know next to nothing about their parents," he informs me.

"Silas? That little traitor. What else did he tell you?" I demand.

"You will never know. I have so much up my sleeve now" he warns.

"I guess I will have to find somebody who knows you too well," I retaliate

"The only person would be Izzy. She has been my best friend for years," he admits.

"I guess I will have to hit her up then." I let him know.

"Good luck, I am always there and y'all won't have a moment alone." He smirks.

"Who said that I need you to be gone for that conversation?" I push. He gives me a sheepish look, a quick kiss, and walks out the door. I have an idea and I can't wait for tomorrow.

# Chapter 10

# Jace

I didn't hear from Ash this morning. Usually, she responds to my good morning text. I just assumed she was running late and hadn't had time to look at her phone. I open the doors to the coffee shop like I do every morning, but she isn't there. Maybe she's in the back.

"Hey, Clara. Is Ash here?" I ask. She shakes her head while she's making a coffee.

"Nope, haven't seen her yet. She called me last night and asked if I would be okay by myself for a couple of hours. Something about having an appointment at the gym?" She responded. The gym, why would she be there? Shit! She's talking to Izzy.

"Thank you, Clara, you're the best!" I yell out while running out the door. I run down the sidewalk, cross the street, and almost got hit, around the corner, and finally, I get to the gym. I try to compose myself before I walk in. Izzy is on the mat, stretching somebody out. I can't see who it is because she is blocking my view.

"Hey, Izzy," I bark out. She turns around, sees me, and smiles. Yup, Ash has to be with her. And I'm sure they are talking about me. I walk up to them and stop dead in my steps. Laying there in black sneakers, tiny black shorts, and a white tank top is my girlfriend. The shorts are showing off her sexy, silky, long legs. Her tank top isn't long enough to touch her shorts so I get to see a sliver of her edible hips. I know what those hips taste like, I have had my teeth sunk in them. Her face is bare and I love that, makeup only covers up her natural beauty. She has small studs in her ears and her hair is in a high ponytail. Fuck, how did I get so lucky?

"Hello, are you in there Jace?" Izzy waves her hand in my face.

"Oh, umm, what are you doing here Ash?" I change the subject.

"What does it look like? You weren't here so I had to get somebody else to stretch me out," she laughs and looks back at Izzy. They both are laughing now and I have a bad feeling I missed out on their inside joke.

"Well, I'm here now, move out of my way." I push Izzy gently. She pushes me back.

"I can't help you were late today, and now Ash here is my new best friend. We love talking about you. I didn't know how little you told her about yourself. It's okay though, I caught her up on everything." She winks, gets up, and goes to the front counter. I look down at Ash, who is staring up at me.

"So, are you going to do it or do I need to get assistance elsewhere?" She's a little feisty this morning, I like it. I get on my knees and pull her leg over my shoulder and start leaning into her. She makes this low groaning noise and

I know she can feel my dick getting hard. I don't even try to hide it from her anymore. It's pointless.

"Okay, I think that's enough. I'm going to go do the leg push thingy." She tries to explain but fails.

"Leg push thingy? You mean the seated leg press?" I inquire, trying to figure out what she wants to do.

"That's what I said. Are you going to supervise me or do you have some other hot chick to stretch?" She jokes. She knows good and damn well that she is the only woman on my brain.

"There's no point in even trying that, Ash. You are the only one that can make my dick this hard. Actually, my dick has never been harder with anybody else. It almost pains me if I don't let him dive into your ocean," I tell her and she turns bright red. I love that I can make her blush like that, it's so damn cute.

"Stop it, we're in public. And there are an unhealthy amount of people here this early," she says as she looks around the room, popping me on the arm. I hold the spot that her hand was on and pretend like it hurt. She knows I don't mean it but she smiles anyway.

"If you haven't noticed, there are earbuds in everybody's ears," I point out. She looks around again and sees them. I'm not going to do anything because there are men here and I don't want anybody to see what's mine. Plus, I don't want them thinking about her while they have their dicks in their hands. I walk her to where the leg presses are and she looks at it for a moment before she sits down. She didn't set the weights, I realize that she has never done this before in her life. I know what's about to happen but I decide not to stop her. She sits back, places her feet on the foot press, and pushes. It goes all the way forward with ease and she's confused.

"So umm, you have to actually set the amount of weight that you would like to push. The machine can't just guess what you want. Here, I'll set it for you. Let's see, hmmm. You can start out with twenty pounds," I educate. Setting it up and taking a step back to watch her. She pushes it with no problem.

"That was easy. Try again," she prompts. I go back to the weights and set it to thirty pounds.

"Okay, how about that?" I try and watch her. Again, she doesn't even strain.

"Do you think I'm a pussy? Give me some fucking weights!" she snaps at me. Okay, so she gets a little rough and competitive. I think I like it as long as she doesn't get too crazy. I set it to seventy pounds. Usually, I don't let anybody jump to that much but she's being snappy. She pushes it again but this time it's a struggle. She barely makes it.

"I guess you shouldn't be a smartass in my area of expertise." I can't hide the smirk when I say it and she glares at me.

"If I wasn't a smartass then I wouldn't be myself. I'm almost positive you like it and wouldn't have got me in that bar bathroom if I was polite." She raises a brow. It's true though. She does ten more pushes and stops.

"Where's your water bottle?" I ask and look around.

"Oh, well you see." She looks to the ground and I catch on.

"You didn't bring water?" I sigh even though I already know the answer.

"No, I didn't think that far ahead." She admits, jutting out her lower lip and looking up at me through her lashes. I go to my locker and grab the empty bottle that I always have in here just in case. I take it to the fountain and fill it with cold water, I walk back to where I left her and hand the bottle over.

"I will never have a problem with you coming here, but what was the mission?" I need to know what she's up to or it will bug me. She downs half the bottle of water before she answers.

"Izzy had some information that I needed. Now we are even with our knowledge of each other." She bites her bottom lip, trying to hide her smile.

"What do you know?" I look over to Izzy, who is watching us and laughing.

"I never knew that you like to dance. She told me all about how you enjoy stepping on toes. I'll have to go out and buy heavy-duty boots." She attempts to keep a straight face but fails and I can feel my face heating. I'm going to fucking kill Izzy.

"I don't do that anymore. My skills are a hell of a lot better than what they were in high school," I clarify.

"Yeah, that was a really long time ago for you, old man." She thinks it's funny.

"You're not that much younger. And anyways, you seem to like my old balls in your mouth," I retort. She throws the now empty bottle at me.

"You're so nasty. Stop it." She looks surprised by my statement.

"So I do have a serious question for you," I warn her. "Why do you not like PDA? Did something happen?" I ask, hoping I'm not poking at a sore spot.

"It's not that I am against it. I've just never done it before, nobody has ever wanted to with me." She shrugs, saying it like it's nothing. I can't hold back, I grab her wrist and pull her up to me, making her body collide with mine. I slam my mouth on hers and tease the seam of her lips with my tongue, requesting entrance. She opens up and starts playing with mine. We keep our dance going for a couple of minutes until Izzy interrupts.

"So, this is cute and all but if y'all are going to shoot a porno, can you at least tell everybody else to leave? I mean, I'm definitely going to stay and have a front-row seat. I just don't think everybody else does too," Izzy says. It takes a lot of effort but I stop eating her face and take a couple of steps back. I look around to see if anybody noticed and stop when I see Ms. Beth staring at us. She has this big ass smile on her face. I can't avoid this now, so I place my hand in Ash's and we walk over to her.

"Ms. Beth, how are you today?" I ask her.

"Skip the bullshit boy, is this her?" Ms. Beth gets straight to the point.

"Ash, this is Ms. Beth, she is my main trainee. Ms. Beth, this is my girlfriend, Ash."

"It's very nice to meet you." Ash sticks her hand out to shake.

"Oh honey, I've been waiting a long time to finally meet you. You are so beautiful. Jace, you never told me she was this pretty." Ms. Beth slaps Ash's hand away. Instead, she goes in for a hug.

"Actually, I do believe I told you that she is breathtaking. Do not try to get me in trouble, I do enough of that myself," I remind her. She just waves me off and goes back to talking to Ash. I have a feeling that they will be here for a while, so I walk over to the front counter and talk to Izzy.

"You actually love her," Izzy says more as a statement than a question.

"Of course I do. I told you that I do." Shocked that she didn't believe me.

"I honestly thought that you would fuck her for a few days and then go to the next," she admits.

"Nah, she's it for me. I love her and her son. I can't fuck this one up," I confess more to her than I have to Ash. I just don't want to scare her off by moving too quickly. I know what I want and it's her. I would marry her right now if I could. She would definitely head for the hills with that one. Izzy's eyes glass up. Shit, where did I fuck up?

"Hey, what happened? Did I say something?" I beg. I don't like seeing her upset.

"You're so stupid. I'm just so happy to see you like this. After everything that fucking cunt of an ex did to you. I love that you found somebody to deal with your shit and love you back equally. You deserve it." She wipes the tears off of her face.

"Awe, Iz, that is the sweetest thing ever. Are you sure you aren't a pillow princess?" I have to joke with her. We don't do this heart-to-heart shit. She slaps my shoulder for that one.

"Shut the fuck up and go run into traffic. You little shit!" She plays.

"What the hell did you do, Jace?" Ash walks up to me. She looks mad. Uh-oh.

"What are you talking about?" Then I notice she is looking at Izzy. "I didn't do anything to her. She just acts crazy sometimes. Don't worry about it." I immediately regret saying that. Ash looks like she is blowing me up in her head.

"Excuse me? Who the hell do you think you are? If that's how you treat your friends, then I don't want anything to do with you. Asshat!" She states in a stern voice. Damnit. I look over to Izzy for help.

"Nope, you called me a pillow princess. I'll let you deal with it," Izzy disengages.

"So not that I called you crazy?" I ask.

"I already know that shit. But don't disrespect me by calling me the feminine type. I am the one that mastered eating. I'm sure Ash doesn't get the privilege of being devoured by a pro." She gives a wink to Ash.

"I handle my business. No complaints and she loves it so much she yells her appreciation." I bite my tongue until I taste blood after that one slipped out. Ash is definitely blowing me up now. Her eyes go big and I know I'm in for some shit.

"We're not even. I have to go to work, I've left Clara to fend for herself long enough. Izzy, kick him in the balls for me, please? Ms. Beth, it was very nice to meet you, bitch at him as much as you can today. Jace, go fuck yourself. Also, I love you and you can make it up to me later. I promise you that I won't be yelling your name anytime soon," she notifies us, gives me an undeserved kiss, and walks out the door. Well shit, that didn't go well. I pull out my phone and shoot off a text.

> **ME: I love you pookie bear.**

> **MY SMARTASS: Don't you ever call me that shit again.**

> **ME: Peaches?**

> **MY SMARTASS: Digging the hole deeper. Keep going and you will be stuck down there.**

> **ME: Fine smartass.**

> **MY SMARTASS: Better. See you later.**

*Hey, at least she is still talking to me. I know I'll get my ass handed to me later but she is still responding.*

"Go ahead and get her some flowers and chocolate. Maybe ask her what she wants for dinner and then you go to her house, cook it and then clean up." Ms. Beth shares.

"Make sure when you give her the flowers, you already have them in a vase. Girls hate it when they have to cut the stems, pour water in the vase, put plant food in, and then shove the flowers in. It takes up time that we don't want to spend," Izzy tells me. Damnit, I just gave her flowers yesterday...with no vase.

"I'm going to have to carry around a notebook so that I don't forget anything. Alright Ms. Beth, are you ready for your session?" I change gears, ready to move on with my day. She looks at me like I'm stupid.

"If you don't get out of here, I'm going to find a cane and hit you with it," she fusses at me. I roll my eyes but smile at her anyways. I go pick up my water bottle that we forgot about on the floor and run out to my car. If I'm going to buy flowers and a vase, I might as well pick up food to attempt to cook tonight.

> **ME: What do you want for dinner tonight?**

> **MY SMARTASS: Hmm, salmon. Surprise me with the sides.**

> **ME: Salmon is your favorite from what I hear. Mashed potatoes too.**
>
> **MY SMARTASS: Don't poison me.**

I don't want to buy any cheap salmon. I also don't know how to shop for food that isn't frozen. So of course, I text Izzy. I really need more friends.

> **ME: Where do I buy good fish?**
>
> **IZ: The fish market.**
>
> **ME: There's a fish market?**
>
> **IZ: Why would I tell you to go there if there wasn't one?**
>
> **ME: Are you fucking with me?**
>
> **IZ: Yes, stupid. We live nowhere near the ocean. Go to the Fresh Market. That is as fresh as we can get. It's in the name. Lol.**
>
> **ME: I swear, stop messing with me. This is important.**
>
> **IZ: I'm serious this time. You won't find any fresh as-hell fish around here.**

I drive to the store and look around. I find an open cooler of food at the back. I see ground beef, steak, and ribs. I go a little further and find the fish. They got cod, shrimp, tilapia, and salmon. I grab two cuts of it, just in case I fuck up the first one. I get some lemons and parsley, I may have looked at Google before coming in. I almost went to the check-out but then remembered the potatoes. I'll need butter to go with it. Shit, I have to do some vegetables too. I heard spinach is pretty good so I'll try that out.

Standing in the middle of the aisle, I try to remember if I'm missing anything. My brain is empty.

Fucking flowers! Shit, I almost forgot. I pick out some carnations that are already in a vase, they are green with white tips. That's a win for me. I feel good about what's in my cart and go pay for it. When the cashier tells me the total, I almost shit myself. How the hell do people cook every day? This is fucking ridiculous. She better love this meal. I pay for it and drive to her house. When I get there, I grab all of the bags in one trip because I'm not a bitch. Once I get to the door I realize I have a major problem. I don't have a key. I'm such an idiot. *Wait, I have Silas's phone number!* I call but it goes to voicemail. Once I hang up, a text comes through.

> **SILAS: At the library. Sup coach?**

I can't ask him to leave. It's education and shit.

> **ME: No worries, I figured it out. Go read or whatever.**

I check the front and back door...locked. I check all of the windows...locked. Damn. I could just break in. No, that's crazy. I don't want to cook it at my house because it might mess up during the drive over here. From what I heard, fish is best eaten when it's hot. I have no other choice, I have to call her. There goes that surprise. She probably thought that I was going to get takeout. I want her to be in the comfort of her home and cook my way into her heart. Plus Silas can eat with us and then go play his video games or whatever he does. I want them to get used to me being around. Giving up on trying to get into the house, I text her. I would call but she might be with a customer.

> **ME: Hey, so can I borrow the key to your house?**

She answers immediately.

> **MY SMARTASS: Are you alone?**

What kind of question is that? Who else would I be bringing over to her house?

> **ME: Of course not! I have the whole damn marching band with me.**

> **MY SMARTASS:** Fuck you. The key is in the backyard, under one of the poles for the trampoline. If you go to jump on it, try to fall off.

> **ME:** I don't know how I got so lucky to be with somebody so sweet.

> **MY SMARTASS:** Go choke on it.

> **ME:** Come on over before Silas gets home and I'll give you something to choke on.

> **MY SMARTASS:** Are you talking about your ego? Because that's the only thing big enough to have that effect.

> **ME:** Big talk for somebody who can't reach the height requirement for roller coasters.

After waiting for another couple of minutes, I figured she isn't going to respond so I go get the key. I let myself in the house and put the fish in the fridge and start looking in cabinets to find a deep pot and a pan. I fill the pot with water and put it on the stove then turn the knob on high. That's as far as I remember from when I pulled up Youtube earlier. I'm glad she isn't here to witness this. I can't even make mashed potatoes without a video. *How am I this old and can't make a simple ass dish?* I pull the video back up and set my phone up. After I start cooking, I realize I didn't get any half-and-half. Fucking perfect. She said she cooks, maybe she has it already. I go back to the fridge and do a little happy dance when I see it front and center on the top shelf. I go back to cooking while I watch the girl on the phone. Only burning myself once or twice but I'm finished and the house is still standing. The kitchen is a fucking mess but I can clean that. I don't think I could have fixed it if there was a fire. I check the time and they should be pulling up so I go ahead and make plates. I don't know what they drink at dinner so I hold off. Ash and Silas walk into the house just as I finish putting the last plate on the table. Silas walks past me but I see the smile he tries to hide. Ash is taking it all in and I'm holding my breath.

"Wow, it looks and smells really good. How did you do all of this when you don't cook?" She asks.

"You don't need to worry about that. Just know that I made it and you won't die." That earns me a smile. She walks up and gives me a little kiss.

"I'm sure it's amazing. Thank you. Let me wash my hands and we can eat. Silas! Come sit down!" She calls.

"I was going to set out the drinks too but I wasn't sure what y'all liked."

"That's okay. We usually just drink sweet tea, I'll get it. You already did a lot, go sit down." She directs, I almost argue but decide to shut up and listen. Silas sits beside me and has this big ass smile on his face.

"Problem?" I urge.

"Nope. I just think it's funny that she has you whipped already. It's been what, a month or two?" He says holding back a laugh and I already know where he gets that mouth from.

"Wow, it's like copy and paste. How does it feel to sound just like your mom?" I bite back.

He rolls his eyes, Ash brings over the drinks and we eat in awkward silence. I can't keep quiet anymore, it's bugging the shit out of me.

"How bad is it?" I ask Ash about the food.

"I've had better." Silas lets his two cents out. I look over to Ash and she gives me the okay to get into this with him.

"I guess you better get used to the downgrade because I will be here cooking more often," I confess and his face is priceless.

"Look, I don't care that you are always around, I'm not even mad at the fact that we will be living together soon. But do not start cooking. I can only pretend that it's good for so long. I mean, I can cook better than this. I would rather eat ramen than your cooking," he pleads and it stings. I look back over to Ash and she keeps her head down, letting us talk this one out.

"What I got out of that little rant is that you are cooking every night. Where is the box to put our request in?" I level with him, I can handle it. He doesn't say anything, gets, up, and places his dishes in the sink softly. Ash must have gotten on him for tossing it in there.

# Chapter 11
## Ash

Jace has been coming over to eat dinner with us every night for the past two weeks. He's been trying to help me cook but he's not allowed to do anything by himself. It was a sweet thought and I love him for it but I can't fake liking it. The boys have gotten along and even go to the backyard to practice with the ball. Their team has won the past two games and they are working together. The game tonight was beautiful. They played like they were in sync. They moved as one and it paid off. As much as I enjoy spending time with my kid, I am in need of some sexy time. We have had sex every day but yesterday. I can't help it, he's so fucking hot. Those abs! His ocean eyes! And his perfect fuck me hair! I have never needed somebody to be inside me this much. I get wet every time I see him, and right now there's a fucking waterfall. He's sweaty and I've been watching him run around for two hours now. I have to have him and I don't think we will make it to his place. Like every other practice and game, Jace waits to be the last to leave. He's so sweet but if we don't get going, I'll show him how naughty I am here on the sideline. Our eyes lock on each other and I give him the signal that I want to go. I can tell that he is struggling to make a decision and apparently so does another parent because the mom smiled and got her son to head to her car. God does love me. I bite my bottom lip and do a little innocent twirl. Jace runs up to me, picks me up, and throws me over his shoulder like a sack of potatoes. I haven't been this happy in a very long time. We get in the car and he drives to his house. I can't stop myself, I loosen my seatbelt and lean over to his lap.

"Ash, what are you doing," he asks but I don't answer because he figures it out when I pull his already hard dick out of his gym shorts.

"I need a shower first, I'm sure I smell bad from running around." Paying his comments no attention, I slowly stroke him a couple of times and then I lick up the side of his hardness from base to tip. After playing with it for a minute, I take him in my mouth.

"Ash," he moans, trying to say something else but he's having trouble. That makes me feel insanely good. I hum a little so that he feels the vibration and brings him more sensation. I feel his hand tug on my hair and that only encourages me to take more of him. I feel the head of his cock touch the back of my throat and I gag. He pulls my hair so that I come up and off of him.

"Nope, we can't do this while I'm driving," he groans.

"Am I doing something wrong?" I have a hint of a whine in my voice because I always think this way.

"The only problem we have here is that I will drive off of this road and hit something. That feels amazing and

I want to really feel your mouth without having to also think about the road. The way your tongue pressed to me while it slides up and down. Mmmm, I can't even talk about it. I already feel like I'm going to cum soon," he explains.

"The way you said that makes me even wetter," I tell him and then grab his free hand and push it down my pants so that he can feel how horny he makes me.

"Shit, Ash. You're so wet for me and I haven't even done anything. Yet. Fuck, I can't wait to taste you," he growls. I pull his hand out and put his fingers in his mouth. I unbuckle my seat belt because we are in his driveway, slide over to him and whisper in his ear.

"How about this? Do you like it? Is it everything you wanted? You do this to me. You make me this way all of the time." I lick the tip of his ear and then my teeth are on it and I tug gently. That's all he needs to get him moving. He takes his seatbelt off, slides to the back of his BMW, and pulls me with him. He lays me down on the seat and hovers over me, putting weight on his arms.

"I'm not on the road anymore. You know what that means," his voice grows dark and husky, it makes my skin rise in goosebumps and causes me to smile.

"Umm, it means your car is in park." Sarcasm is my first language.

"Smartass. It means you are so fucked." He smirks with a laugh underlying his words and before I can comment, his lips are on mine and his tongue is demanding entrance. He kisses me with this needy, primal heat and it just turns me on even more. He pulls his mouth away and nibbles my jaw, down my neck, rips my shirt in half, and stares at my stomach.

"Hey! That was my favorite shirt!" Raising my voice louder than I expected.

"Don't wear shit that you like around me. When you tease me, I have no control over how I get you naked," he says appearing to be in a trance, he lifts my bra up so that he can suck and bite my nipples. He goes from one to the other and then down my stomach, stopping at the waistband of my jeans and snaps the button off. Damn, I liked these pants too. I won't have any clothes by next week if he keeps this up. He pulls his shorts down and goes back to taking my pants off.

"Wait, get a condom," I remind him. Why do I have to keep telling him this?

"I don't have one on me." I push him off of me and pull my pants up. I tie the two pieces of my shirt together and it's enough to cover my boobs.

"No condom, no sex." I make it very clear this time, just in case I didn't before. He pulls his shorts up and gets out of the car. I get out right behind him and wait for him to get the keys out and go to his front door. Once we are inside, he leaves me and walks straight to his bedroom. What the fuck is his problem? I follow behind and he has his shirt off by the time I make it there. I watch him walk to his bedside table and open the drawer.

"What the fuck is your problem?" I lash out, not holding anything back.

"I can't look at you until I get this condom on me because my self-control is very thin at the moment," he says frantically and turns around to me. His shorts are still on but his dick is so big and hard that it looks like it'll rip the front. He clenches his jaw and that's all it takes for my feet to start moving toward him. In one swift movement, I pull his shorts down. I take the condom, rip the foil open and roll it on.

"Now that it's on, what are you going to do with it?" I ask and he smiles. He helps my pants fall down, unties my shirt, and lifts me up by my thighs. He walks me to the wall and slips himself inside of me. He feels amazing and I can't keep my eyes open. My head hits the wall behind me and I moan because holy fuck, I love this man and his dick. I dig my nails into his back and he starts pumping in and out of me. Within minutes, we are cumming together. After we catch our breath, we start laughing. He pulls out and helps me stand because my legs are wobbly.

## Chapter 12

## Jace

"I feel like a bath is in order," I slip the condom off, tie it and throw it in the bathroom trash can. I start the bath and keep my hand under the running water until it comes to temperature. I hear her walking up behind me and then I feel hands on my waist and they slide up to my chest.

"Are you making it hot enough?" she murmurs.

"I mean, it's warm. How hot do you like it?" She drops her hands and I turn to face her.

"Move and let me check it." I watch her ass as she bends over the tub. My dick twitches in response.

"OMG! Do you want me to freeze?" she squeals and turns the knobs to make it hotter.

"What do you mean? That's the temperature I always use." It's not hot or cold, it's perfect.

"If I get in there with the way you had it, my nipples would be razor blades." I walk over to the sink and pull the bubble bath from under the cabinet, walking past her to pour some in.

"Sorry, I should have asked if you wanted to do that. Wouldn't want to do it wrong," I make a comeback and she rolls her eyes at me.

"Stop pouting, it doesn't look good on you." Ouch, but I do feel a bit stupid now. I smile and try to play it off.

"Maybe I just wanted you to make it up to me." I try to bring the situation back to the playful side.

"Make what up to you?" She looks utterly confused, bringing her brows together, tilting her head to the side, crossing her arms, and sinking her weight to her left hip.

"Trying to control everything..." I throw at her and she beams with confidence.

"Do you want me to be in control? I can do that." I don't respond and I guess she takes my silence as a yes because she takes over.

"Get in," she demands and I step in the tub but immediately hop out.

"Are you trying to show me what Hell feels like!?" It's fucking burning. Who can sit in that?

"You're being a baby." She steps in the tub with a straight face and sits, showing no signs of burning or pain. What the fuck?

"You're the devil. Slide forward and let me get in behind you." She smiles and gives me space to get in. "It's going to be really sad when my dick burns off."

"Don't worry, I'll spit on it before it gets to that point." She winks and I sit. Well, try to sit. It is fucking hot! She turns to face me and I wince as I finally get all the way in.

We sit there staring at each other for a minute. I feel her hand grab my shaft. "Just checking to make sure it's still there. We got lucky, Hell isn't hot enough." She smiles and moves to turn the water off.

After it's all off, I pull her to me so that her back is on my front. I lean back to relax and she lays her head on my shoulder. "We don't have anything to wash with." She states and I grab the liquid soap off the side of the tub and squirt some in my hand, rub my hands together until there's a little bit of bubbles. I place my hands on each collarbone and start to clean her. I make my way down to her breasts and spend extra time there. Squeezing and then pinching her nipples. I don't know how to play with the barbell yet but I'll do some research.

I slowly slide one hand over her stomach and stop at her overstimulated clit. I make circular motions with my finger and her hands go to my thighs. My other hand is still pinching and twisting her nipple. "Jace, faster." My dick is now hard and pushing against her lower back. She bites her lip and closes her eyes. It takes me off guard when she pushes my hands off of her and turns to face me. She slams her mouth onto mine, bruising my lips. I feel her grab ahold of the hair on the back of my head and pull. She straddles me and takes advantage of my exposed neck. She nibbles, licks, and sucks.

"Fuck, that feels good." I let my hands rest on her hips. She licks up to my ear and then takes it between her teeth and gently pulls, not much but enough to cause a quick sharp pain. She lets go and licks it to soothe the sting, then her hands drop to my shoulders.

"Grab my ass," she orders and I do as I'm told, again. "Squeeze." Making my nails dig into her, I listen to her take a sharp breath. "Ahhh, yes." She takes my right hand and moves it to cup her pussy, moving her own back to my shoulder. "Dip a finger in." I shove my middle finger into her heat and I close my eyes. Fuck, this girl is perfect. "Open your eyes, I want you to watch me when I cum." I think I might shoot my seed just from those words alone. She starts to ride my hand and it takes all I got not to move and sit her on my dick. "That's it. Fuck!" Her nails scratch and her movements start to get out of control. I use my thumb to rub her clit and that pushes her over.

Her face when she cums is something I need to see every day for the rest of my life. As she rides out the wave, she moans, "You're such a good boy. Showing restraint." I can't hold back anymore, I take my finger out and slide my dick in. Oh fuck me, she feels so good. But then, what I just did hits me. Without saying a word, she stands, gets out of the bath, wraps herself in a towel, and leaves.

*Shit!*

I unplug the bath, tripping on the lip, almost falling on my face. I almost forget about a towel but grab one on the way out of the room. I wrap it around my waist and rush into the bedroom. She's already dressed. She forgot to bring an overnight bag so she uses one of my shirts and gym shorts.

"Ash, I am so sorry. I was worked up and in the heat of the moment, I wasn't thinking," I plead. She doesn't look at me. I fucked up. I knew wearing a condom was a big deal for her. She made that very clear the first time we hooked up.

"Please take me home." *Damnit!*

"We can talk about this." I take a step toward her, reaching a hand out.

"What was the plan there? Get me going and slip it inside without me caring? Are you trying to get me pregnant?" she bombards with question after question.

"Of course not! I would never do that to you," I feel like the floor has dropped out from beneath my feet, my stomach rises to my throat and my words come out a bit more forceful than intended.

"Well shit, Jace! We literally just talked about a condom before we walked into the house. Hell, that was the whole reason why we hurried in here in the first place," she wasn't holding back.

"It slipped my mind!" This time, I meant to yell.

"Slipped your mind," She repeats, rolling her eyes and I know that we aren't getting anywhere tonight. "If something that simple can slip your mind then I'm sure it will be fucking easy for you to forget about me. I don't need you to drive me home, I can figure it out my damn self."

"Please let me take you. I don't want you out in the dark by yourself," I tell her and start putting my clothes on.

"Whatever. I just want to go home." *Fuck, she's never going to talk to me again.* I didn't respect her wishes and now I have to let her cool off. But that doesn't mean I'm giving up. *Oh no, far from that.* I will take her home and give her some space for now. I slip my shoes on and walk out the door. She's already in the car by the time I get there. It was the quietest drive I have ever taken. When I get to her house, I have to tell her how I feel before she goes in and thinks of all the reasons not to be with me,

"Ash, look. I am so sorry. It was a mistake and it will never happen again. I love you so much. Please forgive me. I will prove to you that I am in this with you for the rest of my life. I fucked up and I am so, so sorry." I start tearing up when I get to the end of what I'm saying. Am I really crying right now? I never cried over a woman, not even my ex. I move to get out of the car.

"No, don't." She holds a hand up to stop me and then gets out on her own. I watch her walk in her house and I hate myself. I hang my head and my shoulders drop for a second and think about what I've done. Normally slipping it in without a condom isn't such a big deal but I think there's something deeper going on. I get how she could be upset but not this much. I want to call Silas but that might be overstepping, so I drive away from her and it's really hard to keep going.

I wake up the next morning and check my phone. Nothing. *Shit.*

> **ME: Good morning.**

Nothing.

> **ME: Are you still mad?**

Nothing. Shit. I'm tempted to call but she might still be asleep. I feel like complete shit and I don't know how to fix this. My head and eyes hurt from staying up last night. I got maybe two hours of sleep, maybe a shower will help...

It didn't. I dry off and check my phone before getting dressed. Nothing. I throw my phone back on the bed and put my briefs, gym shorts, and shirt on. I pick my phone back up and decide to call her. It rings and rings, voicemail. I dial her again and still no answer.

> **ME: Very adult of you.**

I regret it as soon as I hit send. Well, just in case she wasn't pissed before, she is now. It can't get any worse so I slip on socks and shoes. Grab my wallet and keys and drive to her house. It was a quick drive and I was a little antsy. When I make it there, her car is gone. I'm still going to knock. After banging on the door a few times, I give up. *Damnit. Where could she be?* The coffee place is closed on weekends and she doesn't hang out with anybody. I'm racking my brain but nothing pops up. Shit. I guess I'll drive around until I see her.

I look everywhere but I come up empty. I try to call her again but it goes straight to voicemail this time. I leave one.

"Please call or text me. I want to talk to you. I'm so sorry, baby. I need you. Please talk to me. You aren't at your house or anywhere in town. Where are you? I will come to you. Please. I love you. So fucking much."

My voice cracks and I can't say anymore so I hang up. I'm on the side of the road and I don't know where to go. My chest aches and I'm pissed at myself. I punch my steering wheel and my knuckles start bleeding but I don't feel anything. "Fuck!" I yell out at nobody in particular. My head hangs and tears fall on my shorts. There's nothing more I can do for now so I go home and clean my hand. I'm not a violent person so I don't know where that came from. The cold water stings but it's deserved. After my hand is clean, I pick up my phone and check the time. I was out there for hours looking for her. I missed lunch but I might as well wait another hour or two and get dinner. Am I even going to eat?

## Chapter 13

## Ash

I spent the day in the next town over because everything reminds me of him. But I'm home now and I can't keep still. Staying here is just sad, I need to go out. Maybe Izzy will want to hang out.

> **ME: Hey! What are you doing tonight?**

> **IZZY: playin around at the bar. what do you have goin on**

> **ME: Can I hang out with you there?**

> **IZZY: hell yes. the only one in town**

> **ME: On my way!**

I could use a drink… or five. I look down at what I'm wearing, jeans, a plain purple shirt, and my Vans, good enough. I don't go over my checklist, I just grab my keys and purse which has my wallet and chapstick in it. Walk out the door and lock it then walk to the bar. I plan to drink my sadness away so driving isn't an option. Luckily it's not far but I am walking the streets at night. So this is a little stupid. It's fine, I'm sure I will be fine.

When I get there I go straight to the bar, order my Jack and Coke and look for Izzy. It takes a minute but I find her. She's in black leather pants that look painted on and a skin-tight white shirt. She is wearing sneakers and the amount of girls around her is crazy. They are all over her. Watching a little longer and I start to feel like I'm intruding on an orgy. She looks up and spots me. It takes her a minute to walk away from the ocean of women but she finally makes it over.

"You seem to be enjoying yourself," I tell her with a little smirk.

"YOLO Bitch." She raises a fist in the air and does a spin with a smile plastered on her face. Her hair is down and wavy, and her face is shiny with glitter.

"First, don't ever say that again. Second, why does your face look like that? You look like you got in a fight with a unicorn," I can't just not say something.

"One of them has a nice rack and I needed to feel them on my face." She gives the most serious face like it's a normal thing.

"So you just put your face in people's boobs all the time?" Trying not to sound judgmental.

"Of course not. She has to have nice big ones that I could have fun with. You, for instance, I would not mess with yours at all…You have nothing there." She smiles when she says it but I know she's being serious.

"Wow. That's ok, Jace likes my… Never mind, it doesn't matter." I forgot why I was here for a minute there.

"Do you want to talk about it?" She leans into my ear so only I can hear, giving me the illusion of privacy. I know she doesn't want to get involved but her being who she is asks anyway.

"Nope. Just want to drink until I feel the need to go home with one of those girls," I open up to her and then take a big, burning gulp of my drink.

"Well then, let's go dance. Bring your drink!" she calls and I follow behind her.

The night is going great and I'm having a blast. Izzy steers away the men, which I requested. I don't want to hook up with anybody, I just want to have fun. After four more drinks, I am grinding my ass on some girl that I've never seen before. Some guys start to come over but I'm too drunk to care.

"Hey, are you ready to leave?" Izzy yells out to me.

"No, this is great!" I yell back. She walks away and I lose track of time.

## Chapter 14

## Jace

I feel empty. My house has never felt this big and empty before. I spent every night with Ash and now she won't even say 'hey' over the phone. Shit. I've been working out so much that my whole body physically hurts. She has taken over my mind and won't leave. Eating hasn't happened, water hasn't either. I keep looking at my phone but those fucking spam calls are the only things coming through. I keep calling her but she keeps sending me to voicemail. I've been sitting on my couch for the past twenty minutes staring at the wall. I can't do this anymore. My phone rings, I pick it up so fast and answer without seeing who it is.

"Hello?"

**"Hey, you're girl is here and it's starting to get a little crazy. I think you should come get her. The men here don't care about shit."**

"Where the fuck is she?"

**"The bar, she's pretty fucked up. I'm trying..."**

I hang up on her mid sentence. I slip on my shoes, grab my keys and wallet and I'm out the door. This is the first time that I intentionally sped. Those pieces of shit better not have their fucking hands on her... I kick up rocks and park in the lot. I don't lock my door, just run through the bars' door and search her out. She's dancing, oblivious to the guys around her. I walk up to her and one of them has the nerve to grab me by the shoulder and to tell me to back up. I push him out of my way, bend to pick her up by her legs and throw her over my shoulders. Nobody says anything as I take her outside. Izzy follows behind me.

"Thank you for calling me."

"Look, I don't know what happened but she came here to have fun, not to go home with anybody. Fix whatever the fuck you did. You saw how many guys wanted to fuck her. Don't give them the chance. She's good and deserves better." She's not telling me anything I don't already know.

"Yeah, thanks again. Did she bring anything with her?" I turn towards the bar.

"Oh, yeah. Her purse is behind the bar. I'll be right back." She runs back in and I take Ash to my car. She hasn't said anything or moved. I open the back door and lay her on the seat. She's passed out. I chuckle under my breath at how fast she fell asleep. It's almost as if she was already asleep on the dance floor. I watch her chest rise and fall over and over again until Izzy comes back with Ash's stuff.

"Here, I don't see her car anywhere, she might have got a ride with somebody." Izzy looks around the parking lot.

I take her purse and look to see if her keys are in there. Wallet, chapstick, keys... My vision turns red. A fucking condom. That better not be new.

"I got her keys. I'm going to take her to her house. I'll text you later." I close the door and jump in my seat. Waving to Izzy, I drive to her house. When I pull up, I go ahead and unlock the door. Less I have to do with her in my arms. Running back, I pick her up bridal style and walk through the door, using my foot to close the door behind me. Still sleeping, I climb the stairs and take her to her room. Laying her on her bed, I take a step back making sure she is still restful. I head back downstairs..

I check to make sure the door is closed and I lock it, take my shoes off and go back to her. She's snoring and it's cute. The sadness hits me because she's not mine anymore. Damnit. I still love her and I'm going to continue to take care of her. I start with her shoes and then her socks. After those are off, I go to her dresser and pull out an oversized shirt but then put it back. I take my shirt off and lay it on the bed, then go back to her dresser to get shorts. Continuing to take her shirt and pants off, replacing them with my shirt and her small navy sleep shorts. I pull the covers out, drag them over and tuck her in. I go back to my car to get her purse. When I walk back into her room, I look for her phone but it's not in her bag. Hmm. Looking in her jeans, I find it in the back pocket. I'm tempted to be nosey but decide against it. I put her phone on the charger and kiss her forehead.

"I love you," I whisper to her and head out the back door to her trampoline and get the house key. Walking back to the house, I lock the back door after me, and head for the front and lock that one behind me as well. I take the key and put it back where I found it and go to my car. It takes a lot but I drive away...

The next day I wake up to no new messages so I send her one.

> **ME: We really need to talk about this.**

> **MY SMARTASS: Sure. Come over.**

> **ME: Getting in my car now. I love you.**

No response. This is going to be a shitshow.

I jump out of bed, put on blue jeans and a black t-shirt and run to my front door. Luckily I sleep with socks on so I just have to slip on my shoes, grab my wallet and keys. I'm out the door and in my car within minutes. I try not to speed but I want to be there like five minutes ago. I pull up to her house and barely close the door before I'm running to her. I knock and wait. It feels like I am waiting hours when really it was only a minute. She opens the door and she's in the clothes that I put on her. Her hair is messy and she must have washed her face because she has no makeup on. She looks perfect.

"Hey," I say simply.

"Come on in," she says and steps aside. We sit on her couch and she takes a big breath.

"Izzy texted me this morning to ask how I was and she said that you brought me home. Thank you." She looks me in my eyes when she said it.

"No need to thank me. I'm always here for you," I tell her.

"Do you know what prepartum depression is?" She waits for my answer.

"No, but I know what postpartum depression is, so I can only imagine. Why do you ask?" I prompt her.

"When I was pregnant with Silas, I was sick constantly. Like really sick. I was also very depressed. I didn't want to get out of bed, I hardly ate, I just slept. My son's father didn't help me with anything. He went to the appointments but he wasn't mentally there. The only thing that I enjoyed was having a baby in my arms. It's very draining and I lost myself. I quit looking in the mirror because I didn't like what I saw and didn't care enough to fix it. I never want to go through that again. The feeling of being worthless and just not giving a shit, yeah I don't want to feel that. It took me months to start caring enough about myself to eat a decent meal. It took years to care about my body. And I still don't care enough to actually work on my fitness. I went to the gym to get your attention, that's it," she explained everything and I feel worse now than when I first got here.

"That's terrible, Ash. I'm so sorry that you went through that. Your ex is a fucking dickhead for not pushing you and helping you take care of yourself. If for some reason we get pregnant, not saying you will change your mind or anything like that but if you do, I will never let you get that far. I won't force you to do anything but I will take care of you and our baby. If you want to take a lazy day, then I will lay in bed holding you all day. If you get sick, I will be there to hold your hair and clean you up. I. Will. Be. There. Please know that. I will always be there for you. It will be exciting and we will celebrate together. I love you and nothing will change that. When your belly swells, my dick will too because you are growing our baby and that is the sexiest thing," I reassure her. She is now letting tears flow and I can feel my eyes start to push one out. I would love to have a baby with her. To have my own kids. But I am happy with having only Silas if that's what she wants. She looks down and shakes her head.

"I'm sure you believe that now but he said the same thing," she whispers.

"I'm going to be here no matter what, I promise." I'm trying to convince her but It's not working.

"All of that may be true but you did something that I didn't want to do. I said it multiple times and I made sure you understood what I was saying," she sniffles and I get it. I messed up.

"I know and I am really sorry. I won't let it happen again. I will be in more control from now on. I promise." She looks down and shakes her head again.

"How can I trust you? If you did this one time, what will stop you from doing something worse? This won't work if there's no trust and right now, I don't have it." Her eyes start to tear up again but she straightens and gets serious. I slide off of the couch and drop to my knees. Moving over to her, I push her thighs apart and sit on my knees between them.

"You can trust me. I won't fuck up again. Please. Don't leave me. I can't, please don't. I'm so sorry," I plead, beg even. I wrap my arms around her waist, drop my head in her lap and start crying. My life is better with her in it. "I will do anything. Whatever you want to prove that you can trust me. What can I do? What do you want me to do? Please," I continue and I mean every word. She looks away for a few minutes and really thinks about this.

"Thank you for coming over. You need to leave now." She doesn't look me in the eyes when she says it.

"What if we don't have sex for a while?" I'm pulling at straws.

"If we do that then what's going to stop you from sleeping with somebody else?" She seriously just asked me that. Really? I get it but what the hell?

"Because I am with you and I don't want anybody else. I don't cheat. Never have and never will. Remember, I know how it feels to be on the receiving end of that shit. Plus, if I just wanted you for sex then I wouldn't be spending so much time with you and Silas. I wouldn't even try to have a relationship with him if that was the case. I fucking love you and I don't say that lightly. I want my future to be with you. You are the only woman that I want to laugh with, cry with, argue with and bitch with. I want your smartass mouth to call me out on all of my shit. So if I need to go back to fucking my hand, then that's what I will do." I say desperately.

"We can't do this anymore. I won't get over it. Without trust, we are nothing. And I don't trust you." She looks away again when talking to me.

"You're ending this? Over something so stupid? You're overreacting." I shouldn't have said that but I did anyways. She pushes me off of her, stands up and is almost vibrating from anger.

"You know where the door is. Leave," she says in a calm, steady voice. There's nothing else I can do, so I get on my feet and leave.

I am going to have to call Izzy to get a little insight. I need to make Ash trust me again. I want all of her and I can't have that right now. I pull my phone out as I get settled in my car and text Ash.

**ME: I love you.**

Nothing. Did I really expect a response? No

I toss my phone on the passenger seat and drive home, thinking about her the whole way. When I make it home I call Izzy.

"Hey Iz, I've got a question."

**"No, you can't stick just anything up your ass."**

"Shut up. I need to make it better."

**"I'm on her side."**

"What can I do to make her trust me again?"

**"Oh no, you did something really stupid. Ok, trust just takes time. But it doesn't hurt to butter her up. Flowers, IN A VASE, bring her food, brush her hair and just help her do things to take the stress off her. She probably has to do a lot since she's a single parent."**

"I asked her to move in with me a few days ago but she shot that down real quick."

**"Y'all have been dating for 2 seconds, why are you asking her that?"**

"I know it seems like things are moving fast but I'm not rushing it. It just flows. I am comfortable around her. I wake up and think about her, I walk around and I'm thinking about her, when I eat I think about her. She's who I think about when I fall asleep. It gets annoying because I just want her to be here, not just in my imagination."

**"That is the corniest shit I have ever heard you say. I don't think you talked like this with that whore you were with."**

"I thought that I loved her but now I know that what I felt for her was nowhere near love. With her, I just liked the idea of having somebody there. But anyways, I won't be cooking for her for a while because last time, they laughed at me. And they hated it."

"I'm sorry, they?"

"Yeah, her and Silas."

**"Wait, you had the kid there with y'all?"**

"Well yeah, I don't just want to fuck her. In order to be with her, her son has to like me. He's a cool kid and I do like spending time with him."

**"Ok, so why did she say no to moving in if y'all are crazy about each other?"**

"I told her the story behind the house."

**"You fucking idiot."**

"I didn't want her to find out from somebody else, then I would have been in deeper shit."

**"If that is what's stopping her, find a new house. It really is that simple."**

"So I will go buy a house and give her the key. I can do that. What do I do about her breaking up with me?"

**"Oh shit. You fucked up so much more that I thought you did. Flowers and chocolate won't fix that."** I can hear her laugh on the other end of the line.

"Women are too fucking complicated."

**"Then go find a man to slip in."**

"I think I will pass on that one. Not saying anything is wrong with it but it's just not for me."

**"Then I guess you need to get over your shit, accept that you fucked up and deal with it. Stop being a pussy and saying how she is complicated. If you want to get her back then man the fuck up. I have to go. I'm wrist deep in this girl's cunt right now."**

"Why the hell did you answer the damn phone?"

**"I had a free hand. Bye."**

I stand in my kitchen and really think about how to fix this. I need her trust before I can even think about us.

# Chapter 15

# Ash

A few days have passed since I saw Jace. I'm dying inside. It wasn't just about him not wearing protection. It was the principle. I said I wasn't ok with something and he did it anyways. What if he is getting comfortable and this is the real side of him? It starts out with this and then he starts doing other things that I am not ok with. I don't want to be in another relationship where I am not respected.

I'm deep in thought when Clara shakes me.

"Hello," Clara says, looking a little worried.

"Oh, sorry. I was somewhere else. What's going on?" I ask her.

"I asked if I could go get some lunch. What can I bring you back?" she questions.

"Oh, nothing. I'm ok, thank you. Go eat something good," I encourage and she leaves. We are actually pretty dead so it's just me with my thoughts. I don't like thinking, it drains the life out of me. That might sound a little dramatic but who is going to judge me? Nobody because apparently coffee isn't a thing today. Which is weird because it is usually on the top of everybody's brain. Maybe I missed something. It is a dreary day. Nothing but dark clouds in the sky. I'm just waiting for the rain to come. I love the rain. I brought my book today so I can sit back and read. That sounds perfect. I walk over to my bag and pull my book out, make some hot chocolate, and then sit by the window and read.

I'm at the heart-dropping part, where the girl does something stupid and tries to get him back by seducing him. Men have tiny brains when it comes to boobs. Just lift your shirt up and they are putty. Well, I can't do that with my ant bites I have going on. I close my book when I hear the door open. Jace is standing there dripping wet. I was so into my book that I didn't notice the downpour. I speed walk to the back and grab a towel. He is standing in the same spot when I get back. I wrap the towel around him to try and dry him off.

"Stop. I brought you something. I was going to wait until this weekend but I couldn't," he says, breathless. Still dripping water all over my floor.

"Ok, well hang on while I get a mop to clean this up," I tell him but he takes my hand in his and keeps me in place.

"I will take care of it. But first, I want you to have this." He pulls something out of his pocket and hands it to me. It's a key.

"What is this?" I'm really not in the mood.

"It's a key to my house," he says.

"Why would I need a key to your house?" I bristle. This is over.

"It's so you can go over there anytime you want. You will need it if I am not home. I want you to know that I'm not hiding anything. You can show up anytime you want and you don't have to warn me," he explains. It takes me a minute to put it together but I get it now. I kinda love that he thought of this. He's trying.

"I don't want you to think that if you get away with this then you can slowly start running over me. That you can do whatever, say sorry and I will melt. I've already done that once, I won't let that happen again," I clarify.

"That's not what I was doing. I won't let that happen again and if for some reason I fuck up again, I will let you walk away. It would be hard and like hell but that's how confident I am that it will not happen." He starts shivering.

"You are soaked," I state the obvious.

"I'm well aware. Please take the key," he pleads and I walk to my bag and pull my keychain out. I walk back to him and let him watch me put it on the ring. He smiles big and I feel like I'm floating.

"This doesn't mean I'm moving in that house with you," I inform him.

"I know. This is just taking the next step. When we live together, because we will one day, I want to pick out a house with you. I want it to be new to both of us and I want you to love it."

"I don't plan to move in with you anytime soon," I tell him.

"That's ok. We have the rest of our lives together. I think I can handle waiting for you," he confesses. This is getting too mushy for me.

"Good, because if you act up again, I will wait until you are on your deathbed to live together." I smile at him.

"Shut up and come here." He motions to me with outstretched arms.

"Umm, fuck that. You are wet," I squeal when he lunges for me. I run to the other side of the counter and he follows. When he reaches me, we both lose balance and fall to the floor. He maneuvers me so that he hits the floor and I land on him. We both start laughing and get caught up in the moment. I lean down and kiss him. Just a little peck at first but then he kisses me and it deepens. Things start to heat up and I forget where we are and literally everything around me fades into the background.

"Ash? Hello, are you still here?" Clara calls out and I'm back to reality. Shit! I get off of Jace and pop my head up from behind the counter. I straighten my shirt and run my fingers through my hair.

"Oh hey, Clara. How was lunch?" I try to distract her from what's in front of her. She just looks at me and smiles.

"Just a sub but the real question is, what did you have for lunch?" she asks, smiling. Jace stands up beside me.

"Well, she was going to have her own sub but lunch was interrupted," Jace told her and I slapped his chest.

"Ouch, that hurt." He feigns injury.

"I'm sorry, Clara. I forgot where I was for a minute," I mumble.

"That's ok. Everybody is probably in their homes anyways. There is a big storm that is coming. Apparently this is just the beginning," she says and my mind goes straight to Silas. I panic and pull my phone out to call him.

"Hey, mom. What's up?"

**"Hey, where are you?"**

"I'm at home. The school said the weather was too bad to stay in. I'm about to take a shower and watch a movie."

**"You can't shower while it's storming. Don't watch a movie that you really like because the power might go out and you will get all pissy that you can't finish it."**

"Ugh, fine. Are you going to be home anytime soon?"

**"I'm closing the shop now. Why? Do you have crazy plans while I'm not there?"**

"Yeah, pretty insane stuff is happening over here. If you stay on the phone long enough, you will even hear the microwave beep. Madhouse."

**"You're such a little shit."**

"You taught me so well though."

**"I'm on my way home. Go to your room if you are going to have your hands in your pants."**

"MOM!"

**"See you soon. I love you."**

"Jeez, I love you too."

I hang up and turn off the coffee machines. Clara washes the pots while Jace cleans the water off of the floor. We finish quickly and lock the place up.

"Do you want me to drive you to your house?" Jace asks.

"I'm ok. This isn't my first rodeo." I beam, confident of my abilities.

"Can I at least follow you home? Just to make sure you make it without any trouble?" he pushes.

"You don't have to but if you want, you can hang out for a bit," I invite him.

"I would love that. But I do need to go home and change. I don't think you want me to sit on your couch with wet pants," he jokes.

"Absolutely not. I will see you when you get there," I'm the last to leave and I turn to lock the door behind us.

"Oh, I'm still going to follow you home. Just because I have to change doesn't mean I will let you out of my sight until you are safe in your house," he says, serious. I stand on my tiptoes and give him a quick kiss. I run to my car and hurry inside. I am already dripping with water in just that short distance. I drive slowly because the rain is coming down hard. It takes me double the time that it usually does to get home and when I do, I don't want to get out of the car. I don't mind getting a little wet but damn. Jace is parked behind me waiting for me to go inside. Ugh, that means I have to go. Damnit.

I grab my keys and my bag and run to the house. The rain is cold and I'm not wearing a jacket or an umbrella. I keep meaning to put one in my car but it never actually happens. Puddles are everywhere and by the time I get to my porch, my socks and feet are soaked. Wet socks are a nasty feeling. It makes me all itchy. Before I open the door I turn and wave to Jace, then I pull my shoes and socks off. I throw them down and go inside, leaving the wetness outside. Silas is standing in the entryway smiling.

"What?" I ask, irritated.

"Nothing. It just looks like you had a crappy day," he says.

"Nope, rainbows and fucking unicorns over here," I retort. He just laughs me off and goes to the living room and watches t.v.. That boy is aggravating sometimes. The floor is now a puddle below me. This day may suck but I still took a step with Jace. That's something. Keep looking at the positive. I'm freezing, so I go to my bathroom and turn on the shower. Drop my clothes on the tile floor and grab a towel to hang up. The water is nice and hot when I step in. My feet tingle from the heat splashing on the cold. I stay there long after I am clean. This is the reason why I can't shower before I have to go somewhere. Walking out of the nice hot water into the cold air is not something I look forward to. Then I think about Jace and hurry out. I hope he's ok. People drive like they are stupid when it rains. I check my phone but nothing new. Getting my mind off of it, I blow dry my hair and put on my gray sweatpants and a black T that says 'Book Boyfriends Do It Better'. I check my phone again and there's a new text message.

> **ASSHAT: I'm leaving my house now. I'll paddle my boat there as fast as I can.**

I don't text him back because that would distract him from the road. I double-check the timestamp and it was three minutes ago. He should be here soon. I get a couple of towels and take them to the front door. I soak up the water up from when I walked in. The other towel is for when he gets here. I forgot to let Silas know. So I hurry to his room and knock on his door. I've already learned my lesson from just walking in. That is definitely a bad idea.

"Come in," he calls through the door and I open it but don't walk in.

"I just wanted to tell you that Jace is coming over," I notify him.

"He's not going to cook, is he?" he asks.

"I really hope not. But it's not even close to dinner time," I tell him. We laugh and I leave him to whatever it is he was up to. I don't even want to know. There's a knock at my door and I jump in excitement. I run to open the door and almost trip over my own feet. I catch myself and take a deep breath. I open the door to a very sexy Jace. He also has on gray sweatpants but he has on a red shirt. He was smart enough to use an umbrella. He has common sense, that's not something most people obtain.

"You made it," I state the obvious.

"Hell or high water baby." He smirks. I can't believe I let him go. I just shake my head and step to the side so he can come in. He drops his umbrella on the towel and takes his shoes off. I close the door behind him and he gives me a soft kiss on my cheek.

"Silas is here," I remind him.

"I wasn't going to throw you against the door and take you. Calm down ma'am, I am a respectful gentleman," he says placing a hand over his heart, and I can't hold back the laugh.

"Since when? You haven't been decent since I've met you." I laugh as I say it.

He whispers in my ear, "You like it when I treat you dirty. I think that you would even beg for it." And he just walks away. He leaves me standing here with my jaw dropped and thighs wet. So he wants to play, good thing I'm in a playful mood. He goes to the kitchen and fills himself a glass of water, making a show of it. I watch his Adam's apple bob while he swallows. When he finishes it, he pulls the bottom of his shirt up to wipe his mouth. His abs are on full display and I'm walking over to him without even thinking. I bend my knees so that I'm in a crouching stance and lick him from the waistband of his pants to his nipples and circle them. Most men aren't into that but the way his breathing picks up and the bulge pressing on my abdomen, he likes it a little too much. I step back and pull his shirt down, smirk and walk away.

*Game on, bitch.*

The afternoon goes by insanely slow. I keep watching the clock waiting for it to become late enough to send Silas to his room. Jace has been pushing himself on me and grabbing my ass when he passes by. He even licked my neck while I was making tea. I have been working him up as well. Every so often I will have to pick something up while he's behind me. So, of course I would have to bend over to get it. I like to listen to him growl and groan when my ass presses against him. It was a long tit for tat. I'm so horny that if my pants were just a little tighter, the seam would make me cum.

A plan pops in my head. I'm going to fuck with him even more. It will be fun but it will also show me if I can trust him the way that I want. When the day is finally done and the sun is set, we talk about dinner.

"Sorry man, but there is no way in hell you are making me anything," Silas says to Jace.

"Silas! Watch your mouth. You know not to cuss around me just for the fun of it. Be respectful," I tell my son.

"It's a good thing I wasn't planning to cook," Jace tells him. So this is what it's like to have more than one kid in the house. I'm going to lose my mind.

"It's ok boys, I was already planning to make spaghetti. Go watch a movie or something together," I wave them off to the other room. I get started on cooking the meat and I hear them yelling. What the hell? I run to the living room and they have soccer on the t.v..

"If he would have ran the play like it was planned, he would have scored," Jace yells at Silas.

"Sometimes you can't do everything that's planned. Sometimes you have to think on your feet," Silas retaliates.

"Look at number 8. He doesn't even know what he's doing. Stop standing around and kick the damn ball," Jace shouts at the game. Nope, this is not for me. I go back to the kitchen and finish dinner.

The game is almost over when I set the plates on the table.

"Food is done," I call out but they don't move from the couch. Pick your battles, Ash. This one isn't it. Fuck it, I'm hungry. I sit down at the table and eat by myself. Their food can get cold for all I care. Once I'm done, I clean up my spot and go to my room. Five minutes later there's a knock on my door.

"Come in," I say loudly. Jace walks in.

"Sorry about that. We got caught up in the game and I wasn't paying attention," he admits but I am feeling a little petty.

"Yeah, you seem to do that a lot," I snap.

"That's not fair. I apologized for that and it will never happen again. But getting caught up in something like that, especially with Silas, it's most likely going to happen again. We were having a great time together and I wasn't going to walk away," he explains to me and I feel stupid, yet again.

"Your food is getting cold," I dismiss him. A few minutes later Silas yells through the door.

"Goodnight mom."

"Goodnight," I say back. Good, now that he is gone to bed, I can finish playing with Jace. I pull out my vibrator and strip down to nothing. I lay there waiting for Jace to walk in. He knocks instead.

"Can I come in?" he calls.

"Please do but you aren't allowed to touch me," I tell him as he opens the door. He steps in the room and closes the door quickly, then locks it. I turn my vibrator on and start playing with myself. Jace is trying so hard to stay on the other side of the room. He pulled his pants down and he's stroking himself. That sight alone has me coming undone.

"Oh, Jace. Yes. Fuck me," I moan out but he knows that it isn't permission to move. After I finish I get up and clean my little companion off, put it back in my drawer and act like nothing happened.

"Did you need something?" I look at him waiting for an answer. His eyes turn dark and I can tell he wants to pounce. He doesn't say anything, just stands there holding his dick. It's my turn to take some control. I get so close to him that I can feel his heat but not close enough to where we are touching. He moves to grab my hips but I catch his arms and move them above his head. I walk him back to my wall and push him against it, hard.

"Keep your hands up just like that. Don't move," I demand. My hands explore his hips, moving up to his abs.

"Damn, I love how in shape you are. These abs are so fucking sexy," I praise. My fingers linger on his stomach a little longer and then move up to his chest. I remember how he caught his breath earlier when I licked his nipple, so I do it again. He clenches his jaw and I run my hand up his chest to his neck. I squeeze just a little and bite his chest. He moans in pleasure and I want him so bad at this point but I want to play with him a little longer. Keeping my hand on his neck, trailing my mouth to the side and bite. He growls and that makes me even wetter. I straighten myself and look into his eyes.

"I like when you growl." I get closer to whisper in his ear. "It's incredibly hot," I give him another praise. Then I reach down to my pussy and feel the wetness. I shove my finger in me so that I can have it soaked with my juices and I put them in his mouth. "Suck," I simply say. He does and groans in response. "Do you like the way I taste on your tongue?" I ask him.

"It's my favorite flavor," he responds in a husky voice.

"That's too bad because I want to taste you. Do your arms hurt?"

"Yes, a little sore," he says.

"Good, stay like that," I command and drop to my knees. I put my hands on his thighs and keep them there. I lick his hard dick once and then take him in my mouth. I bob my head back and forth as fast as I can with no hands. He makes little noises and it encourages me to keep going.

"Fuck," he groans under his breath. I let him drop out of my mouth and look up, licking my lips. He stares down and he looks like he's going to explode any minute now.

"You taste so good." I get to my feet and up on my toes. I bite and lick his neck.

"Good boy. Now I'm all yours but you know the rule," I point a finger at him to remind him, and not even a breath later he picks me up by my thighs, I squeal but wrap my legs around him. He turns and pushes me against the same wall and nibbles on my ear down to my neck.

"I've learned my lesson, condom always." He resumes his onslaught on my neck and then takes me to bed, drops me, and goes to get a condom out of my nightstand. He puts it on quickly and flips me over so that I'm on my hands and knees. He slaps me on my ass, hard. It's the bite of his hand that has me moaning.

"One day, I want this ass. But right now I am going to fuck your pussy hard and fast," he teases me and I'm squirming my ass against him. Without warning he thrust himself in me. "Fuck, you're so tight and wet," he groans out.

"Only you get me this wet," I confess and it's the truth. I've never dripped on my sheets before. After that, he fucks me so fast that I can hardly catch my breath.

"Shit... Jace... Oh my god," I scream out. His hand goes over my mouth.

"Shh, you better be quiet before the house hears you," he whispers in my ear. He keeps his hand over my mouth and the other on my shoulder, pulling me back as he pushes in me.

"I'm going to cum," I breathe out through his hand and the next second we are cumming together. He pulls out of me and slaps me on the ass again but not nearly as hard. I fall flat on my bed and try to catch my breath. He walks into the bathroom and then comes back to me, condomless.

"That was so good," I pant and he smiles.

"Yeah, it was. Thank you." I'm confused.

"For what?" I ask.

"For letting me have another chance to prove myself to you," he answers and I hold back my tears. Nobody has cared this much about me before.

"Thank you for not giving up on me," I tell him. He looks at me like I'm insane. He lays on his side, facing me and cups my cheek.

"I will never give up on you. What we have is everything to me. You are everything to me. I love you" he confesses and this time a tear escapes.

"I love you too," I say back and the power goes out. I hear Silas yell at something. Probably his game. Now that he doesn't have power, he's going to wallow around. Good thing it's time to go to sleep. I get up and put on my pajama shorts and a large shirt. I walk to the bedroom window and look out at the rain.

"It's raining harder than when you fuck me," I joke with Jace. He wraps his arms around me from behind and kisses my neck.

"Bend over and I'll show you how much harder I can go," he teases and I laugh.

"I don't think so. My vagina hurts already. I'm going to be sore for days," I admit. I feel his smile on my neck.

"Now you will remember that you are all mine," he growls and that earns him a big ass smile me. We stand there watching the storm for a while and I start to doze off. I feel him pick me up and carry me to the bed, pull the sheets over, and climb in beside me. After that, I pass out.

# Chapter 16

## Jace

I feel somebody on top of me and I open my eyes. Ash is naked, straddling my hips. My dick is hard in her hands and she is stroking me. She spits on it and it's the best thing. After a minute of her playing with me, she slides down my legs and leans down to take me in her mouth. I'm hitting the back of her throat and she's swallowing me down. She's making all the right noises and she's about to milk me when something hits me. What the hell? I'm so confused. Something hits me again and again… My eyes open fast and wide. Ash is hitting me with a pillow. She's smiling and beautiful.

"You woke me up from a damn good dream," I say and tackle her so that she is now laying under me.

"Oh I know. You were moaning and I was scared to touch you because I thought you would cum. But you do look delicious. Maybe I could get a little taste." She starts trying to bite my arm but it's just out of her reach.

"Ooh, it's too bad you are so tiny. Are you going to work today?" I'm not sure if the power has come back on but I'm sure she has already figured it out.

"Nope, the lights are still off." She shakes her head.

"Did you try to flip the switch?" I can't help but fuck with her.

"Well shit! I guess I never thought of that. Thank you for having such a big brain." She gives it back to me.

"From what you have told me, my brain isn't the only thing that's big." I smile while I take in her features.

"You're right. Your ego is also pretty huge," she's always got something to say back. I love that she doesn't just take it but gives it back to me just as hard.

"I want to try something with you today." I'm a little nervous to bring it up but I really want it.

"Ok, what ya got?" She looks confused when she asks.

"I want your ass," I simply say, very nervous at her facial expression.

"Is the regular way not good?" she prompts but not in a way that says, I'm in trouble.

"It absolutely is. I just wanted to try something new. I want all of you. Every part of your body and maybe you will even allow me to share my name. I don't know, just a thought." I'm slowly regretting adding that last part in. This is probably the wrong time.

"I haven't had any good experiences with that. The butt stuff, I mean." She looks uncomfortable talking about it but I can't make her feel better about it if I don't know what went wrong.

"Ok. Can you explain a little bit more? What happened?" I don't mean to overload her with questions but I gotta know.

"Well, I only tried it once and it hurt pretty badly." She starts to fidget while she explains.

"It hurt? Did you use enough lube?" I hear that if you do it wrong, it can be uncomfortable but it shouldn't hurt.

"Lube?" She looks confused.

"Yeah, you know the wet liquid that usually comes in a clear bottle." She has to know what that is, she is definitely old enough to have had that in play.

"Yes, asshat. I do know what it is. He didn't use it at all. He just kind of pushed himself in and it burned and was very painful." She is really nervous now because she won't even look at me while she talks.

"So that's not how it's done at all. No wonder why it hurt. Dude was a fucking idiot. How about if I ease you into it? Not put myself in you but start out with some toys," I suggest and she looks shocked.

"Oh, I don't have any toys like that and if you have some, I would rather not use them." She's so serious.

"Crazy but I don't randomly have butt plugs hanging around my house. I meant I will order some off the internet. Brand new, never been used before." I laugh when I tell her about it. She gives me this eat-shit look but I can't stop snickering.

"Fine, you can buy them but don't push me." She looks like she's really thinking about this.

"I promise we will take it very slowly and I will get everything to make it as comfortable as possible," I say and kiss her cheek. We lay on the bed cuddling each other and at some point we fall back to sleep. When I wake back up she is still sleeping. I quietly walk to the bathroom to pee and wash my hands. She is still asleep when I walk back so I check my phone.

> **IZ: You better have straightened your shit up.**

Leave it to Izzy to get me straight. After telling her about me fucking things up with Ash, I took her advice but then I just stayed to myself. She texted me a few times but I didn't say much of anything. My nerves had me by my balls.

> **ME: Yes, I begged and pleaded. We are ok and I am still making it up to her.**

> **IZ: good, so you are alive. i was looking for a spot to bury you.**

> **ME: Haha. You are hilarious. Almost made me think about smiling.**

> **IZ: i like her. better not fuck it up again or I'll break up with you for her.**

Yeah, yeah. I won't mess it up again and if for some stupid reason I do, I'll give her everything in my name and walk away. I look down at her and think about how lucky I am to have such an amazing woman. My phone is almost dead so I put it back down on the bedside table. I walk over to the window and look outside. The rain has stopped but the yard and road areis flooded. I guess I get to stay here even longer. I can't make her any breakfast with no power. Shit, I bet everything in her fridge is ruined. I open it and just like I expected, it's warm. The milk smells bad, there's some nasty shit floating in the orange juice. Guess I better get to work. I get a trash bag and start filling it up. I pour the milk, juice, and tea down the drain then throw the containers in the bag. Next, I'm looking in the drawers. This is what happens when the power is out half the day and all night. Ash isn't up when I finish up so I decide to get a Clorox wipe and clean up the now-empty fridge. When I am almost done, I hear footsteps behind me. I look over my shoulder and she is staring at me.

"Everything went bad so I took care of it," I say and then stand up to face her.

"Oh, that sucks. Now I have to stock up again. Thank you for doing all of this. You didn't have to." She wraps her arms around my neck.

"If we were living together, which is what I want, I would have done it anyways. I just pretend that I stay here." I lean down and give her a quick kiss.

"I love you, asshat." She thinks she's cute.

"I love you too, smartass." I squeeze her in a tight hug and kiss the top of her head.

"Oh, God. Jace, I can't breathe. Let go,." she is grunting but she can breathe just fine. I drop my arms anyway.

"Are you trying to say that I'm incredibly strong?" I joke with her and flex my biceps. She burst out laughing and then I spot Silas walking around the corner.

"Good morning sleepy head." I welcome him. He still looks half asleep and maybe a little irritated. He must not be a morning person.

"It's hard to sleep when I have to have a pillow over my head because people can't shut up. Did y'all remember that I was here? Or did you just not care?" he asks and I see his mom's smart mouth come out in him. Ash starts to say something but I put my hand out to stop her. The boy needs to grow up and not be sheltered to everything.

"Sorry, Ash. But if I could take this one." I look at her instead of just jumping to it. She motions for me to go ahead. Alright, here we go.

"Yeah, we just didn't care. Thought about settling down but then I thought better of it," I tell Silas. He looks even more pissed and it is a little funny.

"You're an ass," he snaps at me and rolls his eyes.

"That was a great job with the grammar. Most people would just call me an ass. You called me an ass. Good job, proud of you." I stare at him and smile. Oh, he is definitely blowing my head off in his mind right now. He gives me a disgusted look, rolls his eyes, and goes back to his room.

"You can't be a dick to him. He's only fifteen," Ash jumps in.

"Actually, he needs somebody to set him straight. You coddle him, which is great and all but he needs some toughness too. I'm sure his dad does great with him but he doesn't show it around me. I want to be a part of his life but I don't want to be a doormat for him to walk all over. If you really feel like I need to back off, tell me and I will." I'm hoping she doesn't take any of that the wrong way. She's usually pretty understanding. She huffs out some air and thinks.

"Just don't cross the line of being a careless dick that needs his ass kicked. I will let him do it with no punishment." She gives me a smirk but I know she's not joking. That's ok because I won't let it get that far. I know how to walk away when needed.

"Yes ma'am." I lean down and give her another little kiss. I let go of her and go back to cleaning the fridge. While I'm doing that, she is cleaning the stove and counter. I thought it already looked pretty good but I guess her standards are higher than mine. I will have to step it up. She's used to doing everything herself and I know she can do it but I don't want her to have to. I want to be the one she can count on. It takes us about thirty minutes to finish up and we go to lie on the couch. There's not much to do but cuddle and talk. After a while, she gets bored with it and goes to get a book.

"What are the naked firemen up to these days?" I remember her reading that porn at the first practice. She hops on the other end of the couch but I can't have that. I move closer and lay my head in her lap.

"Actually it's naked doctors now," she corrects. It's all the same to me.

"So cliche. Are they falling for their patients?" I ask like I know everything but really, I looked that shit up on the internet.

"No. It's actually one doctor and two patients. There is no love in this one. Just filthy, kinky sex. The places where they do it are crazy but it's so hot. And the way he takes them. Mmmm." She is practically moaning as she talks about it.

"Maybe I should taste you while you read." I am actually really excited to try it.

"No sir. We already traumatized Silas for one day. But that is very intriguing. I will have to remember that the next time the house is empty." She is basically drooling over the thought. I try to fix myself before she sees how hard that made me but I'm not quick enough. She doesn't say anything, just smiles at me, and then goes back to reading. I'm actually really comfortable and I feel myself slowly falling asleep while listening to her breathe.

It took three days for the water to disappear. I'm glad that I got to spend time with Ash but I need a shower and clean clothes. The power came back on this morning and Ash was really excited to go to the store to get real food. I think we are all tired of peanut butter and honey sandwiches. I wanted jelly but that was one of the cold things I threw away. I told her that I would enjoy grocery shopping with her if she could just wait for me to take a warm shower. She had the same idea but her shower will probably be scorching. I still don't understand how she can handle that. Does she just not like her skin and wants to burn it off? It's so weird but Iz says that every woman is like that.

"I'll call you when I'm on my way back. Don't melt in the fire that you call water." I add that bit because it's been way too sweet between us lately so I need to balance it all out.

"Maybe you can stop being a pussy and take a real shower," she says so seriously. I would have thought she was mad if she wasn't pretty much jumping up and down, excited to get clean. She's crazy.

"I love you." I kiss her and she hums in approval.

"I love you too. Make it back to me." She's been on edge a bit since she heard about all of the people that didn't make it home from the storm. It was really sad and it hit too close to home.

"I will always make my way back to you," I reassure her. I give her another kiss and walk to my car. The drive home was depressing. Trees were torn down and there were houses that got hit hard. It makes me feel terrible. I hate seeing these kinds of things. When I get home, I go straight to the shower. As I wash myself, I think about all of those families and their homes. I want to do something but what can one person do? I'll have to go ask around to see if I could maybe try to rebuild a house for them. I don't know but I know for a fact that I can't stand around and do nothing. With the idea in my mind, I get out of the shower and wrap a towel around my waist. I go get my phone and remember that It's dead so I plug it in and get dressed. By the time I am dressed and have my shoes on, my phone is charged twenty percent. Not much but it's something. I text Ash. She might still be in the shower so I don't want to call.

> **ME: I have an idea for the town. Tell me if it sounds stupid.**
>
> **ME: What if we build them new homes? They are almost all torn down from the storm and the flood.**
>
> **ME: Never mind, it's probably stupid.**

**MY SMARTASS: I love it. Where do we start?**

> **ME: Really? Do you want to do it with me?**

> **MY SMARTASS: Of course I do.**

> **ME: I fucking love you.**

> **MY SMARTASS: Ditto.**

Ditto. She's going to get her ass popped. Oh shit! Today is Saturday, game day. I call the rec to see if it's still on but they said that with the ground still having water, it is delayed. Good because we have hardly practiced this week. I send out a mass text to the team's parents updating them. Half of them don't and the other half respond with a simple ok. The season has gone by fast and now that the moms have left me alone, it has been smooth. I pack a bag to keep in my car just in case I stay again.

> **ME: I'm on the way over.**

> **MY SMARTASS: Ok, be careful.**

I drive a little under the speed limit because there are still a lot of puddles in the road. It takes double the time to get there. When I get there I see Ash pacing on her front porch. Oh shit. I hurry out of the car and run to her, splashing the whole way. She stares at me with wide eyes and then jumps in my arms. There are tears in her eyes and she's sniffling.

"What's wrong? What happened?" I'm rubbing her back and trying to get an answer.

"I thought something happened to you. You said that you were on the way almost twenty minutes ago. I was so worried." She has to take breaths between each word. She was worried about me? I didn't think it would be a big deal.

"Shhh, it's ok. I'm right here. I'm ok." I continue holding her and rubbing her back. Her sobbing slowly comes to a halt and then she takes her hands and pushes my chest.

"Next time, call me! I was so scared and I don't like it!" She looks like she's going to slap me but that would be a big mistake.

"I'm really sorry I didn't call. Next time I drive slowly, I will let you in on it. Promise." I kiss her forehead and smile. I hate she was so worried but at the same time, it feels really good. She calms down and I wait for her to get herself together.

"Ok, I'm good. Let's go inside, I don't want the neighbors in my ass." She turns and walks inside without another word. When we get settled on the couch, I pull her into my lap. I kiss her neck and down to her shoulder. She shrugs me away.

"What's wrong?" There's no way she is still upset.

"We can't do anything right now." I'm confused by this. She's never pushed away from sex with me.

"We don't have to do anything. Just hanging out is perfectly fine. Just curious, why?" I don't want her to think that we have to have sex every time we are together. But I'm nosey as hell.

"Because while you were gone my body decided to let mother nature take over." I don't want to sound stupid so I'm not going to ask but I'm at a loss. She can tell because she rolls her eyes. "I'm on my period, stupid," she clarifies and honestly, I should know that. I do know what it means when a girl says mother nature. Sometimes I just go stupid around her. She is probably thinking that I'm a complete dumbass.

"Do I look like a teenage boy? Don't answer that because I know you are about to be a smartass. A little bit of blood doesn't bother me." I try to make up for my error.

"It's not a little bit on the first two days." Every female is different and I need to make note of what her cycle is.

"This is going to sound crazy, tell me if you heard of this one before, there's this thing called a shower and it is where you can clean yourself," I say to her and she slaps my shoulder....again. That seems to be her thing.

"That is crazy. I didn't know you knew about that magical place, ya know since you stink all of the time." This woman likes to tease.

"Smells bad...hmm... Is that why you like to put those lips on my dick and moan while you're blowing me?" That made her face pink up and her eyes go wide. I love that color on her.

"Jace! Silas is in the next room, be quiet." She looks towards the hallway to see if he's there but I know he isn't because I keep checking.

"Come on, let's go. Plus I would actually be helping you out more than anything so I will be waiting for a thank you." I throw that little piece at her, I have some knowledge.

"And what the hell would I be thanking you for exactly?" She thinks she's got me in a corner.

"Sex helps with the cramps and the mental state. It's the answer for everything actually." I school her. Well, kinda. She gets off of me and turns to leave. When she gets to the other side of the living room, she stops to look at me.

"Are you coming or do you just enjoy teasing me?" she says with that cute smirk that makes my heart fly. It's also making my dick stand up right now. Of course, I jump off the couch and walk to her.

Monday morning comes around and I'm back at work. The field was dry this morning when I checked it, so practice gets to start back up and I'm excited. It's been too long since I wore my cleats. I don't miss it enough to change last Saturday though. After Ash got comfortable with being in the shower with me while she was bleeding, we couldn't get off of each other. We had sex three times, we washed each other while I gave my dick time to get hard again. The only reason why we called it quits after the third time was because the fucking water went cold.

"Jace, are you training me today, or are you going to stand there and stare? I know I look good but you can't have me." Ms. Beth is a trip. She came in earlier than normal today. She claims that she feels her muscles slimming down. I think she was just tired of being in her house. She's not like other older people. There's not a day that passes that she isn't out and about.

"Damn, I was really hoping that you would give me a shot." I smile at her and she rolls her eyes.

"How is it going with that girl of yours?" she asks.

"Ash? We are good. Actually, better than good. I'm really happy. I started looking at houses to show her. I've been wanting to live with her but the house that I bought for my ex isn't going to cut it." I've looked at six houses but they haven't felt right. I'm starting to get aggravated with it. Maybe I should just tell her. We are going to end up in one house in the future so why not move the date to sooner.

"Good. I'm happy for you. Don't fuck it up again." She's not like the other old ladies that I have met. She's doing free weights and there's no struggle. She's wearing her bright pink shorts and highlighter yellow shirt. Her shoulder-length, straight gray hair is brushed back into a low ponytail.

"You know, if the weights are too light you need to get the next one up. If you pushed yourself as hard as you pushed me, you would be stronger than everybody in here."

## Chapter 17

## Ash

Like every Monday, it's stupid busy here. Most people are regulars and they order the exact same thing every time. Every once in a while there will be new people but that's rare. I wish they would try something new. It gets boring to make the same coffee over and over. I might start forcing new things down their throats. After two crazy hours, it finally dies down.

"Hey, Clara, can you hold down the fort for just a little bit? I have to run an errand." It can wait but I'm too excited.

"Yeah, no problem. Enjoy yourself and also eat something." She has been reminding me to eat lately because I keep forgetting. I blow her a kiss and walk to my car. Well, skip to my car. When I start driving, I try not to speed. It feels like it takes forever but I finally pull up in the Lowe's parking lot. I get my keys and purse and head in. I go straight to the key maker and pull my key out. I don't want to make a regular copy. There are a few designs that I can choose from. Hmmm. Do I go with the bright pink or the kitten... maybe the unicorn? But then the perfect one jumps out at me. It's black with three pink hearts on it. I put my key in the hole, (that's what she said) pick the design and pay for it.

It takes about two minutes and the new key pops out. He's going to love it. I go back to my car and drive to his house. When I get there I just sit in my car for a few minutes. I haven't been here without him before. I'm actually a little nervous. I take a deep breath and get out, walk to his front door, and unlock it. Stepping in and closing the door behind me, I go to his kitchen and put the key on the counter. He has to have the paper somewhere for me to write a note. I look around but come up empty-handed. Really, who doesn't have a notepad? I find his mail and turn one of the envelopes over and write on the back.

Here, now you can just walk in and take me.
If you don't then I will take all of your briefs
and hang them up all over town. So you better
use it and fuck me in the middle of the night.
I love you asshat

There, that should do it. I leave the key and note and go back to the coffee house. The parking lot is packed. Shit. I run inside to a stressed Clara.

"I'm so sorry. I didn't think we would have a rush right after the first one this morning. Where do you need me?" I ask Clara. She just looks over at me and smiles.

"You know that you are the boss, right?" She has a point but that doesn't mean I'm going to be a bitch.

"Obviously but you know what's going on right now better than I do so again, where do you need me?" She is slowly calming down.

"Can we do our usual?" she asks. When it gets busy she takes the orders and I make the drinks. It runs smoother that way.

"What's the first drink," I start.

"Mr. Fletcher." That's all she has to say. He comes in every day wanting a black coffee with four ice cubes in it. He says it cools the coffee to the perfect temperature. Whatever floats his boat. We get through this random rush and I notice that it is already past lunchtime. I notice Jace sitting in a chair by the window. I stayed back to take him in. He's wearing black gym shorts that stop right before his knees, a tight white undershirt and his hair is messy.

He sees me and his jaw clenches. I feel the wetness between my thighs. It happens every time I see him. I try to control myself but fuck it. He's my man and I want to show all of the girls in here. They come in here all the time looking for him. Now that he's here they are hiding behind their coffees. One of the blondes gets up from her table and walks over to him. Nope, not today sweetheart. I go to him, throw my leg over his waist and straddle him. I grab his hair and pull his head back so that he's looking up at me.

"You're mine. Better remember that." And I bite his bottom lip before I basically eat his mouth. I come up for air and lick the side of his face. I believe I got my point across so I get off of him and walk back to the counter. I don't hold back on the smirk when I see the girl looking at me. Her face is priceless. It's like she's pissed, in shock, and sad all at the same time. Luckily I don't give a shit about her feelings. It would be great if she got mad enough to never get coffee from here again. When she stomps away I look back at Jace. He's smiling and I notice the bulge in his shorts. Yeah, my mouth is going to be all over that when the shop closes. Jace comes up to the counter and lightly lifts my chin up so that he can kiss me softly.

"One day I'm going to take you right here on the counter. The practice has that fucked up for today but I will make it happen soon," he whispers.

"That would be a big violation with DHEC." I point out even though that sounds so hot.

"We will just have to sneak around and then scrub the place down. But I will be sliding inside of that slick, tight pussy of yours in this building." His words have me crossing my legs just so the tension can be relieved. I need to look and see if his gym is open all of the time because I want to bend over a weight bench right after he finishes a workout. He will be all sweaty and sticky. Normally I would think that to be disgusting but when it's him, oh I have wet dreams about that almost every night.

"I'll see you at practice. Try not to slip and fall into one of those girls' vaginas please." I smile and wink at him.

"It will be rough but I'll try my damndest," he jokes back.

"I love you asshat," I tell him as he walks away.

"I love you too, my little smartass." And he walks out of the door.

"Excuse me but what was that?" Clara pops up behind me. I forgot that she has been here.

"Those whores have been eyeing him for weeks now. I just wanted to make it clear that I will knock them on their asses if they try something." I definitely made my point.

"So you piss on him like a dog? You can't mark your territory like that." She acts like this actually involves her.

"I guess it's a good thing that I didn't pull my dick out. That may have been crossing the line." I feel attacked so I walk away. I've learned to not stay around when I get even the slightest bit irritated. I don't want to say something that will mess up our friendship just because I got heated up at the moment. I step outside to get some fresh air and take a few breaths. The street is busy and the heat outside is starting to get irritating. I get that I live in the south and all but why does the Spring time make me want to jump in a pool? I complain every year and every year I say that I'm going to move north to the cold weather. But I never do. I can't get my sweet tea up there and I'm sure I'll start hating the cold after a while.

For some stupid reason, I decided to wear jean pants and a t-shirt today. Won't be making that mistake again. I wonder if I could control myself around Jace when he's outside shirtless, hot, and sweaty. I wouldn't put money on it. I decide to go back inside before I make myself wet with need. I'm calm and smiling when I face Clara. She smiles back and I guess we are going to pretend that didn't happen. Fine by me, I can't stay irritated with her for long anyways. I look up at the clock, we have five minutes before we close up.

"Go on, and head home. Thank you for everything today." I start to wipe down the tables while she gathers her things. I really do need to hire more people. Clara shouldn't be worked this much. She says she has no problem doing it and it actually gets her out of the house but it still feels wrong. I walk her out and lock the doors. I still have to clean the coffee makers and balance the register. We close earlier on the days that Silas has practice, luckily his games are after the normal closing time. I'm deep in thought when I hear my phone ring. Jace.

"To what do I owe this honor?"

**"Is anybody else there with you?"**

"I don't know if I want to tell you. That sounds creepy as hell."

**"I try. May I please come in?"**

I look over to the door and he's standing there watching me through the window. Fuck this.

"Sorry, but I don't like this. I will see you at practice."

**"Wait, wait. I didn't mean anything by this. I was just trying to be romantic. You liked it when Ross did it to Rachel at that cafe she worked at."**

"That was completely different. They just had a fight inside that cafe two seconds earlier."

**"Please, just let me come in."**

I hang up on him and walk to the door. We just stare at each other through the window for a few seconds and I unlock the door and step aside.

"Lock it back or people will come in," I tell him as I walk back to finish cleaning the pots.

"I'm sorry that I freaked you out. That wasn't my intention. I was going to fuck you on every surface in this building. At this point, we won't have time for that." He says and I whimper. I look back at the clock and decide that we are good on time. I put everything down and turn to jump into his arms. He catches me with no problem. He doesn't even grunt.

"We may not have time for every spot but we can get in a couple."

Practice ran longer than it normally does. Jace had already warned me about it. Since they haven't been on the field in a week he wants them out there as long as possible. Some of the parents were getting antsy but the kids loved the time they had. I kept quiet in my seat until a mom yelled at Jace to hurry up because she has things to do. I stand up real fast and walk over to her.

"If you can't let your kid have time for sports then why did you sign him up? Was it because it distracted him from whoever you've been talking to on your phone every practice and game? Oh yes, I did notice that. How about sit your ass down and let them finish. Tell the person that you are talking to, they will have to either wait or you can go buy a damn vibrator like the rest of us." I act like that didn't take every bit of confidence I had but really, I'm scared out of my mind. I don't like standing up to people but at the same time I am not going to allow a bitch to talk to my man like that. I can't stand this lady anyways, she always acts like she is above us. Screw her. She doesn't say anything and I am so grateful because I don't have any more in me.

"Ok ladies, settle down. Practice will be over in ten minutes. The boys are really into this and I didn't want to stop it but I will so that everybody can get on with their lives. My apologies for keeping them so long," Jace calls out from behind me. I'm so confused about why he is sorry. He walks back to the team before I can ask about it. I go back to my chair and pull my book out. Fine, I'll just get lost in the classroom where Mr. Fisher is getting his dick sucked by the straight A student. She must be really good at it. There's no way I could do the things she did, or even look good in one of those schoolgirl skirts.

It does get me thinking, I want to go out and get the perfect outfit for one of these nights with Jace. I don't even know what he likes though. If I'm going to spend that kind of money then I'm going to get something that makes his jaw drop and his dick stand. Silas runs up to me and takes me out of my thoughts. Has it been ten minutes already? That went fast, I didn't even get to read. Silas helps me out of my chair and folds it up.

"Can I have the keys?" He is a little on edge.

"What's the rush?" I don't mind him going ahead but it seems odd. He shifts back and forth between both feet.

"Nothing. Can I have them or not?" No, he didn't. I stand up straight, push my shoulders back and look him dead in the eye.

"You can watch your attitude or you can walk your ass home. And don't even think about asking somebody else for a ride." I don't mean to be a bitch but I will not let my kid run me over like those other parents that I see on t.v. do. He doesn't respond but he looks over my shoulder and just stares. I turn around to see what the hell has got him so worked up. A short, curvy girl with long blonde hair. She's flawless and I'm not going to lie, I'm kind of jealous. I wish I looked like that at her age, hell, I wish I looked like that now. I turn back to face my love-struck son.

"Why aren't you going over there to talk to her?" I ask the obvious question.

"I can't. I mean, look at her. She's perfect and beautiful and everything. I will just look stupid. They will laugh at me," He whines. Nobody likes a baby.

"Y'all leaving?" I hear Jace ask before I see him.

"Yes, because Silas is too scared to talk to that girl over there," I explain to him. He looks over at the girl and then back to Silas.

"Do you want my advice?" Jace looks to Silas.

"Nope, sure don't," Silas quickly responds.

"Good, so here it is. Walk over there and introduce yourself. Don't shake her hand, that will make you look like you just want to be friends." He gets interrupted.

"I definitely said no." Silas huffs but Jace ignores him and finishes his speech.

"Look her in her eyes and smile. Not a stupid smile, you don't want to give off creepy vibes. Ask her if she likes books. She looks like a reader. When she asks you what you like, don't lie. Just say that you want to pick up something new and if she has a recommendation." Jace finishes. I'm actually stunned that he knows any of that.

"Is that how you met mom?" Silas asks him. Jace and I both start laughing.

"Nah, that's not quite what happened. But I did learn a lot about her when we met." I want to slap him for that. Hopefully, my kid will never know that story. That would scar him for life.

"Go ahead, we will be right here waiting when you are done. And just to answer the question before it's asked, no you can not go home with her." I have my serious face on now. Even though he stopped listening to me once Jace walked up. We stand back and watch as Silas goes to claim his love. Or whatever bullshit the kids call it these days. I feel a hand on my ass and I look up at Jace.

"My favorite part on you." He smiles and squeezes.

"Somehow, I'm not surprised." I roll my eyes.

"Which brings me to something I want to ask you." He looks nervous which makes me nervous in return.

"What?" I just want to hurry and get to the point.

"I want to try something with you this weekend," he says and I already know it is a sex thing. Anything else can happen when Silas is in the house but only crazy sex things happen when he's gone.

"I'm scared. What is it?" I nervously ask. He lightly slaps my ass and smiles. Ugh.

"What is it with men and butt stuff? Is my pussy not tight enough for you?" I groan.

"Oh no, don't you turn this on me, ma'am. You are enough in every way. But you do have a nice, round ass I want to bite. And if I'm biting it, I might as well stick my dick in there." He smiles and whispers back. Silas comes running back to us with a big ass smile on his face.

"That makes no fucking sense." I finish that conversation off right before Silas gets to us.

"Just act cool, walk to the car," he pants while he passes us. Well ok then. Jace and I give each other a quick look and decide to not look back at her. He walks me to my car in silence, holding my hand. It's a small thing but the simple hand-holding makes me melt. Once we get to the car we stop and stare at Silas. Waiting.

"So what happened, man?" Jace quizzes him.

"She gave me her number." He is trying so hard not to jump with happiness.

"That's awesome. I told you, I know how to do this. Just hang with me and I'll show you all of the tricks." Jace smiles when he says that but I have to burst his bubble.

"Um, sir. No. You are not one to teach anything because our meeting was terrible and the second time we talked was also bad."

"Really? I actually remember it very differently. From where I stood, literally, you voiced how much you liked our running into each other. Am I mistaken? Maybe we should try it again just to see if anything has changed." He smirks and I'm sure he is happy with himself right now.

"This got weird. Can we go home? I'm hungry," Silas speaks up.

"Yeah, get in the car and we can go home," I tell him as I kiss Jace bye. He pulls me in for a deeper kiss.

"I love you," he says, still on my lips.

"I love you too." I lick his face.

"I will never wash that spot again. You will forever be on my face." He is something else.

"Maybe I'll sit on it later since you like it so much." I escape his hands and get into the driver seat before he can get to me again. I blow him a kiss and he catches it. Sometimes we are super cheesy but whatever.

"Can you stop? It's getting old," Silas whines.

"You should be happy right now. That girl has an interest in you. Watch and learn, sweetheart. I know the way to a girl's heart, not Jace." After I said that, I drive off to the house. How can I be head over hills for somebody that I just started seeing two months ago? This is crazy but I don't want it to stop. I need a woman to talk to. Izzy told me we should hang out while I'm sober one day. Apparently, last time was too much for her. I don't even remember that night. I wonder if she could be a friend. The car ride was quiet and once we got home Silas ran to his room.

"SHOWER!" I yell so he can hear me. He better not lay on that bed while he smells like that. I stand there and wait for the sound of the shower starting. Once I hear it I take my phone out of my back pocket.

> **ME: Hey!**

I put my phone on the counter and start dinner. When I say –start dinner– I mean heat up pizza rolls in the microwave. They taste better out of the oven but laziness just hit me. My phone beeps with a text message after I put the plate of food on the table. Tonight is more of a one plate and we both pick off of it kinda night.

> **IZZY: sup girl**

She doesn't use punctuation. Good, I don't have to spell everything out and use proper grammar.

> **ME: I need a girl to talk to about Jace. Would it be weird for you?**

> **IZZY: spill!**

**ME:** I'm insanely in love with him but it's too soon to feel that…right?

**IZZY:** do you take years to hate somebody

**ME:** No. I don't like them as soon as they open their mouth

**IZZY:** so why cant you love somebody that fast

**ME:** I never thought about it like that

**IZZY:** im a genius

**ME:** Definitely.

**ME:** Izzy doesn't use capital letters, punctuation, or really anything grammarly correct.

**ASSHAT:** Nope, she is smart but she says that it takes up too much of her time that she could be knuckles deep in somebody.

**ME:** Hmmm.

**ASSHAT:** Don't you dare.

> **ME: Will you help me fuck with Jace?**
>
> **IZZY: i love it what do you want to do**
>
> **ME: Are you busy or can we meet up somewhere?**
>
> **IZZY: shes asleep. where do you want to go**

She's going to walk out on somebody while they sleep? I get it now, she's doing the fun part of being single. I respect that.

> **ME: It doesn't matter, I just want a picture of you kissing my cheek or something.**
>
> **IZZY: why not your mouth**
>
> **ME: I don't want to push my luck and make him mad.**
>
> **IZZY: i got you**
>
> **ME: Do you want to meet at the gym?**
>
> **IZZY: hell yes. be there in 10**

> **ASSHAT:** What are you planning?
>
> **ASSHAT:** Why are you ignoring me?
>
> **ASSHAT:** I'm calling Izzy.

> **ME:** Calm down and keep your belt buckled.

> **ASSHAT:** I don't wear belts but I will go out and buy one right now to use on you.

> **ME:** Daddy?

> **ASSHAT:** I wish I was into that because it would be hot but I can't do that. It's like me calling you mommy.

> **ME:** Eww, totally different. I have a kid that calls me mom. Hard pass.

Fifteen minutes later I pull up to the gym to see Izzy already there. I guess I did leave later than I planned. She is cute though. Skin tight black leather pants, white shirt with a deep v-neck, black leather half jacket, and black heels. I'm second-guessing my sexuality right now. I get out of the car and walk to the gym door where she is.

"Damn. You look hot." I don't even try to pretend that I'm not thinking it. "If only you had a motorcycle."

"Who says I don't? I can't drive it in heels. Come on, I brought you an outfit." She catches me off guard with that.

"An outfit? For what?" I'm utterly confused. I just wanted a funny picture.

"Yes, Jace will love it. After many years of being his best friend, I have learned he likes almost the same things I like. Well, when it comes to what our women wear at least. As far as sex goes, I like mine on their knees. Jace likes them to take control over him." She sounds like she has experience with that and I don't like it.

"Have y'all ever....umm..." I don't want to say it out loud because I know it's a stupid question.

"Girl no. I'm strictly kitty. I tried fucking men before and it feels good but I don't get turned on by them. Dicks are not appealing to look at. Plus women know what women like. I would rather be eaten by somebody who knows how to read the map without a GPS. We have been close friends for years now, I talk to him about my sex life and usually he talks about his." My eyes go wide after she tells me that. "Don't get your panties in a wad, he hasn't said anything yet." That gives me some relief and I do feel better about her.

"Ok, so what will you have me wear?" I submit because why not? I'm already here and there's no turning back. She just gives me a smile and walks into the building. I follow her back to the girls locker room. She hands me light blue jeans and some black lace.

"Is this it? Where's the shirt?" I'm a bit scared now and all she does is a wink at me. She walks out of the room and I strip down. I no longer care if anybody walks in. Holding up the black thing, I don't know how to put it on. It's a one-piece but there are so many strings and holes. I turn it over, nope. I turn it around the other way, nope. What in the actual fuck? Who wears this shit? I lay it out on the bench and stare. Still completely naked, and still haven't put underwear on.

After a couple of minutes, I figure it out. The boobs part is thin silk and the rest is thin silk fabric strings. It's barely covering anything. My stomach is showing, my back isn't covered and it's a spaghetti strap. It's a onesie thing and the back is going up my ass crack. Again, why do people wear this? I put the jeans on and walk in front of the mirror. Oh my damn. Wait, I look good. I get it now. Fuck comfort, looking this good is worth it. I wish I had bigger boobs to fill it out but other than that, yes. I do have a small pouch but I never wanted a six-pack or anything. I also really like late-night snacking. Chips taste better when it's dark and I can't see how much I'm eating. Izzy is letting me keep my shoes which I'm happy about because she wanted me in heels. No way on God's green earth.

"Yes ma'am! Look at you. I would do you." Izzy walks in with her phone in hand.

"Are you taking pictures of me?" I secretly like it but I let people believe that I don't.

"Hell yes, I am. When we finish tonight I will send all of these to you. Send a little bit at a time to Jace." She is loving this and I think I am too. I may even get them printed out if they are good.

"So why am I all dressed—" I look down at myself "—down?" I really just wanted one picture to be funny.

"I want to do a photoshoot. Come on, I want you on some equipment." With that said, she walks out. I didn't sign up for this. But I follow her anyway. If she says Jace will like it then I will give it my all. She stops at this machine where you bend over the bar and push your leg up behind you. There's a bar that goes over your leg that you have to lift.

"Get up there and bend over." I do as she says. When I am in the position she comes up behind me and pulls my pants down, just under my ass. I move around the way she tells me to and she positions me on different things throughout the gym. Luckily there is nobody here except the one guy that works here. Izzy told him who I am and who I am dating. The guy walked off somewhere and I haven't seen him since. She told me I don't have to worry about him sneaking looks. He knows Jace will beat the shit out of him. Oddly enough that turns me on. My man fighting for me. Sounds bad but nobody can read my mind. When Izzy is happy with her work she does a selfie of her biting the bottom of my ear lobe. She sends it to me and I immediately send it to Jace.

> **ASSHAT:** Hey! That's my ear! I'm the only one allowed to bite it.

> **ASSHAT:** What are you wearing? Send me a video. I want a full circle.

Izzy looks at the messages and laughs.

"Why is his name asshat in your phone?" she asks.

"When we first met, that's what I called him. He calls me a smart ass. It's our little thing." I can't stop smiling.

"That's sickening in an adorable way. I would like to be at y'alls wedding. I'll wear a tux and be on the grooms side. I don't do the whole dress thing, sorry." She is out of her mind.

"Who said we are going to get married?" I haven't told Jace that my feelings are that strong. They are but I haven't voiced them.

"Have you seen the way he looks at you? And the way he has been driving himself crazy trying to find the perfect house for y'all," she says.

"Wait, what? He's been looking at houses?" I knew he wanted to live together but he didn't tell me he was looking for a house yet.

"Oops. I'm not sorry though. He has looked at so many houses but they haven't been up to his standards for you." She keeps talking but I get lost in my own thoughts. He wants it to be perfect. Hmmm. I have the perfect idea!

"I'm going to change and then I have to go." I race through my words.

"You can keep those, I'm sure you will be wearing them again." She laughs and walks away. I run to the locker room and hurry out of this contraption and throw my comfy clothes back on. Much better. I gather everything and run out of the room. Izzy is standing by the front counter waiting.

"Hey, thanks for everything. Sorry but I can't hang out, I have an idea and I need to go look into it." I try to catch my breath. It's funny that I have this super fit boyfriend but I am so out of shape.

"Go on. Have fun," she yells out at me but I'm already out the door.

## Chapter 18

## Jace

I look over her note for the millionth time. I gave her a basic ass key and she turns around with a fuck me note and a key designed for me. I need to step up my game. My phone beeps with a text message.

> **MY SMARTASS: I have an idea.**

> **ME: That's never good.**

> **MY SMARTASS: Shut up. Never mind, I will just get a house built for me then. Since you're going to be a pain in the ass, you can't live with me.**

> **ME: Calm down. There is no need for crazy talk.**

**MY SMARTASS:** I was thinking after we help fix that house the storm fucked up, maybe we can get somebody to build us one. What do you think?

**ME:** Why don't we just build it ourselves?

**MY SMARTASS:** We can but it will take longer to finish because we both have other jobs.

**ME:** I can get some people to help. I think it will mean more if we do it together.

**MY SMARTASS:** Have you talked to the people to see if we can help with their house?

**ME:** They said that they are hiring somebody but we can help if we want to.

**MY SMARTASS:** Oh, if they have a team doing it then I would sit this one out. I don't want to get in the way of professionals.

> ME: True. Did you have fun with Izzy?

> MY SMARTASS: Sure did. She really opened my eyes to new things.

> ME: That doesn't sound good.

A picture comes through of Ash straddling a bench with round weights sitting in front of her. When did she get that outfit? I have to get her to wear that for me one night. Her jeans are loose but everything else is tight. The black top doesn't cover much and I imagine running my tongue over every open part.

> ME: Fuck. You are sexy.

> MY SMARTASS: I'm glad that you finally figured that out.

> ME: The things I would do to you in that.

> MY SMARTASS: Please share with the class.

> ME: Are you wanting phone sex? I can do that but you can't touch yourself just yet.

> MY SMARTASS: That's just mean.

Another picture comes through. This time she's bent over with her pants down and she's looking back over her shoulder at the camera. I decide two can play that game so I take my shirt off and put one hand behind my head. I make sure to flex my muscles when I take the picture. I send it to her and wait.

> **MY SMARTASS:** That is now my lock screen. Thx.

> **ME:** Am I just now stepping up to wallpaper status? You have been mine for over a month now.

> **SMARTASS:** You just haven't been worthy.

> **ME:** Wow, I see. Hang on.

I jump out of bed and go to my dresser. I have a silver chain necklace that I haven't worn in a while. I put that on and get back in my bed. I sit on my knees and set my camera on a timer, lay the phone down, and hover over it. One hand is on the headboard and the other pushes the circle for the timer to start. When it starts I place my other hand on the bed beside my phone. I wanted it to look like she is under me. My chain is hanging and I don't look half bad. I get why girls love this position but I don't understand why there has to be a necklace. It does nothing but get in my way. The picture snaps and I send it.

> **MY SMARTASS: That one will be printed and hung on my ceiling. Then I can fuck myself while I look at you.**

> ME: Hold on now. Just call me over and I can be there in person. I'm better than any of your battery friends.

> **MY SMARTASS: Izzy made a good point tonight. She said women know what women want. It's too bad you can't step up to knowing how to do what I want.**

> ME: I know what you want. You want to be spanked like you've been bad. Your hair pulled like you're looking up to pray to Jesus. You want to be fucked hard and thrown around like it's nothing.

> ME: I bet that made you so wet that you had to touch yourself. Tell me, with your fingers deep inside that sweet pussy, are you dripping?

> **MY SMARTASS:** Yes.

> **ME:** Can you do the job or is your pussy yelling out for me? Is it craving my dick to fill it?

A picture message pops up. I open it and fuck... She's completely naked. Her back is arched off the bed and her toes are curled in the sheets. She is holding a vibrator that looks like a bullet in one hand and the other is playing with her nipple. I rub my dick through my gray sweats and imagine it's her.

> **ME:** You fucking tease. I have a picture of you cumming now and I will use it often. I want to be licking up every bit of that sweetness. Tell me I can come over.

> **MY SMARTASS:** You have a key dumbass.

That's all the permission I need. I don't respond, just get out of bed and slip on shoes. I don't bother with a shirt, I need to feel her warmth around me. I get my wallet and keys and leave, locking the door behind me. As much as I want to, I don't speed. It's taking too long to get there. I have the urge to cum but I push that feeling down. When I get there I grab the box of condoms I keep in the console and run to her door. Not walk but literally run. I know what's waiting for me in there and I want it bad. I use the key that I put on the keyring next to the key for my house. It's dark and quiet inside. I close the door behind me and remember to lock it. I'm pretty good about being safe. I quickly take my shoes off and walk to her room. I don't knock, just walk in. She's in a short red silk robe that barely covers her ass.

"Fuck." I can't think of any other words. All of the blood has run from one head to the other and I can't think clearly.

"Close my door," she says and I do as I'm told, not looking away from those dark eyes. "Get up here." She doesn't have to tell me twice. I start to pull down my pants but she tells me no. "Keep them on." Whatever she wants. I climb into the bed with her and she pushes me back to lie down. I like where this is going. She throws her leg over me and straddles my hips.

"Somebody wants attention," she moans and circles her heat over my hardness. "Are you going to be a good boy for me?" She asks and damn, this is going to be a fun night.

"And if I'm not?" I want to see how far this is going to go.

"I won't give you what you want most." She thinks she knows all of me. I'm afraid not.

"What is it that you think that I want?" I question her. She smiles and runs her soft hands up my chest and stops at my neck. Her fingertips press a little harder than she normally does. She leans down to where her hand stops. Her tongue darts out and the pressure makes me tighten my jaw. She licks from her fingers up to my ear. When she gets there she bites my ear lobe, hard. Not hard enough to draw blood but enough to show me that she is in charge.

"I know what you like. What you want. What you need. You want to be in control but you need to submit sometimes. This is the time. Be good and I'll let your finger explore whatever hole you want," she whispers and shit, how did she figure it out. I told her about my neck but I never admitted to needing a break from being the man that takes care of everybody. I want somebody to take care of me.

She lets go of my neck and her fingers play in my hair. She pulls my head back and captures my mouth with hers. She bites my bottom lip and pulls a little. There's a sharp pain but I like it. She lets go and licks it, soothing the burn. She crawls over me far enough that her boobs are on my face. I grab her ass and suck on her nipple. She gives a low moan and crawls up further. She doesn't stop until she's sitting on my face. I grab her thighs and pull her down farther. My tongue touches her and she trembles. I devour her like she's my last meal. She's so close and she starts moving her hip to ride my mouth. I try to keep her still but damn, those thighs are powerful.

"Fuck...Oh, My God! Jace, yes! More pressure. Stop playing with it and eat me!" She tries to be quiet but fails miserably. I slide my teeth over her bud and that's all it takes for her to go over the edge. When she finishes her orgasm she tries to get up but I hold her to me. My tongue stays on her and she starts to giggle.

"Stop it. It tickles." This time I let her go. She moves off of the bed to go to her nightstand. I don't see what she pulls out but she has a questionable look on her face.

"You're making me nervous. What are you hiding," I ask her and she walks over to the foot of the bed and crawls on.

"I'm just in the mood for strawberries." She shows me what she has and it's strawberry-flavored lube. I have never experienced it before. She grabs my dick through my pants and moves her arm up and down, toying with me.

"You're going to kill me." I can tell my voice is a bit strained. I'm so hard that it nearly hurts. She has a wicked smirk and slowly pulls my pants down. I lift my ass off of the bed so she has no problems and once she has them off, she pours a small amount of the liquid in her hand. Rubs them together and slides them on my shaft. It's warm and a bit tingly. She leans down and licks it off.

"Oh fuck," I whisper. I don't know if it's because I think this is erotic or what but either way, I like it. She licks all the way around and then plays with the head. I start to move my hips and thrust to get into her mouth but she's not having that.

"How did I piss you off?" That's the only explanation. She has to be making a point that I'm not getting. She doesn't say anything while she climbs off and goes to get a condom out of the box I dropped on the floor.

"I'm not mad. I just wanted to play. It's just an added bonus to watch you squirm." She's evil. It all makes sense now. I close my eyes and try to think of anything else in the world so I don't cum without even being touched. I feel her rolling the condom on and then there's nothing. I open my eyes to make sure that she is still there.

"Would you like me to finish this or do you want to participate?" She gives me the opportunity and I am not about to pass it up. I sit up, pick her up by the underside of her thighs and throw her on the bed. In one quick motion, I hover over her and thrust myself into her. I don't stop or take it slow. I have been patient but now... now I get to have her. Her nails are clawing my back and her feet are on my ass, pushing for me to go faster.

"You feel so good! Don't stop." She starts getting loud again.

"I'm going to put my dick in your mouth if you don't shut up." Outside of the bedroom that would have gotten me to hit but in here, she eats it up. Her mouth finds my shoulder and her teeth bite down. It gives me a tingling pain but that only adds fuel to the fire. I speed up and all I can hear now is the slapping of our skin. I want to last longer because she feels so damn good it's not going to happen.

"Fuck me like you mean it," she whispers and that sends me over.

"Shit. Neck, neck." That's all that I can get out but she understands what I want. She quickly grabs my neck and presses her fingers on the sides to where she's not touching my windpipe. I get lightheaded but it's enough to have me cumming hard. She lets her hand fall to my chest and I pull out of her. Slowly she sits up and winces.

"Did I hurt you?" I look her over to make sure I didn't leave any obvious marks.

"Only in the best way." She giggles and kisses me. A light, sweet, tender kiss. We lay down beside each other and try to recover.

"Great. Now that y'all finished that disgusting crap, shut up next time. Or even better, wait until I'm not here," Silas yells through the door.

"Shit. I fucking suck as a parent." Ash beats herself up too much when it comes to her being a mom. I get out of the bed and take the condom off, tie it and throw it in the bathroom trash can. I find my pants and pull them up.

"Where are you going?" She looks confused.

"Was this not a booty call?" I give her a deadly serious expression and her eyebrows go up. "I'm going to talk to Silas. But then I'm leaving. I don't want you to think that every guy will just hang out and cuddle after a late night sex thing." I wink and smile.

"I'm not the one that likes to cuddle after sex. I like my space. You are the one that has to suffocate me," she quips back. I just keep on smiling and walk out of the room to go find this kid. I go straight to his room and knock on the door. His bed squeaks and he's grumbling about something. The door opens and he has this weird smell going on. Ash might not know what it is but I have had the same smell in my room while I was single. I look over his shoulder and yep, lotion and a shirt beside it.

"Hi," is all I say because really, how do you start this kind of conversation?

"What do you want?" He's so grumpy.

"I had sex with your mom." I'm not being a dick but he needs to grow up a little.

"Awesome. Anything else?" He's a little smartass.

"Did you know that she had to do the same thing with your dad to make you?" I know that he knows but I'm getting to a point.

"Is that how babies are made? Had no idea. Thanks for letting me know. See you later." He is his mom's son. Fuck this kid.

"She has sex. It's a part of life. But you should know all about that part seeing how you do the same thing to yourself." He goes to look over his shoulder but then stops himself.

"I'm not stupid. Nobody wants to hear their mom. It's disgusting. Next time, just shut the hell up," he mutters and pushes the door to close it but I stop it with my hand.

"Were you listening? Is that why you're all set up over there?" Yeah, ok. That is nasty to think about but I want him to open up to me. His mom can't help him with this knowledge.

"Are you fucking sick? No, I wasn't listening. I had my headphones in, looking at my phone. I took them out because I had to go pee and that's when I heard y'all. When I got out of the bathroom everything was quiet. That's when I yelled through the door," he explains and that's my window.

"What website were you on? You are in the Incognito mode, right?" I don't really care what he looks at but he needs to know how to hide that shit from his mom.

"The what mode?" He is in desperate need of a real male figure. His dad is obviously failing.

"It's where you can search things without it showing up in your history. Seriously? Step up, man." Talking the cool lingo is not for me anymore. I'm too old for this shit. "I'm not going to hold your hand through this. Look it up on your phone. Thank me later." And with that said, I leave him to it. That was very uncomfortable but it had to be done. I couldn't just let him hear me fucking his mom and not work things out with him. He would have been all pissy for days.

What the hell is his dad even teaching him? Educating kids about sex is one of the basics, especially for teenagers. Has he even had the talk? Would Ash have done it? I open the door to Ash passed out on the bed. She put on tight little pink night shorts that could pass as underwear. Her black shirt is two times bigger than her. There's a pillow between her bent knees and her arm is under the pillow beneath her head. She must have been really tired to fall asleep that fast. The covers got messed up during our little cardio workout. I reach down and pick the sheet and comforter up and gently lay it over her, trying not to wake her. There's something shiny on the floor that catches my eye. I bend over to investigate. Oh, it's just the condom wrapper. I pick it up and before I stand there's something under her bed. I don't want to be nosy but all of the best things are hidden under the bed. I get down to my knees and pull the small white box out. I hesitate but only for a second before I pull the lid off.

This takes me by surprise. I never thought I would see this around her. I wonder how long she's had it. Three black silicone butt plugs in different sizes, a bottle of water-based lube and a small purple vibrator. It's a starter kit. She's been getting ready for me. I close the box and push it back where it came from. I slip into the bed and pull the covers over me. The damn pillow between her legs is getting in my way. I pull it out and throw it on the floor. Sliding my leg between hers and arm hugging her waist. I can get used to this. It wasn't on my agenda but I can be ok with surprises like this. I would have been home thinking about her anyways. She wants to build a house with me. This is a dream, it has to be. I'm a 35-year-old soccer coach that has nothing going for me but a pathetic job at the gym. I thought my time with finding love was over. But she walked in my view and I was proven wrong. She's perfect. I lay there with my eyes closed, feeling her chest rise and fall. I don't know when but I fell asleep.

There's yelling. Who the hell is here this early? I open my eyes and remember that I'm at Ash's house. I look around and she's not there. I force myself out of the bed to see what the problem is. When I get to the living room, Ash is standing there with Silas's father. What the fuck.

"So that's it then, you're just going to fuck your son's coach? Is that giving him more game time? Is that why you are doing this, so Silas can sit on the bench less?" Dipshit has some nerve.

"Can I help you with something?" I step up to him. He doesn't cower but he doesn't take a step either.

"I don't want my son around some guy she is whoring around with." He is out of his damn mind.

"It's fine, Jace. Just go back to bed." Ash tries to push me back to the room.

"Did you just call her a whore? I can't be hearing that right." Somehow I stay calm but his face is pissing me off.

"I mean she's fucking you to get something out of it. Call it whatever you want but it's not real," He spits out.

"Oh, I get it now. You don't understand. When people, like Ash and I" – stepping back to get in his face — "fuck as hard as we do, it's so that we can cum. Did you know that she can do that too? I bet you don't even know how sexy she is when she gets to that spot right before she explodes. I bet that you have never given her one." I forget about everything around me.

"Jace! That's enough," Ash yells. I may have gone too far but I have no regrets. I step away from him and I don't try to hide my smug smile. This guy is a piece of shit, he never deserved her.

"What's going on?" Silas pops up. He's so quiet that I keep forgetting that he is here.

"Nothing. Go back to your room," I bark before Ash gets to it.

"Don't fucking talk to my son like that. The same kid that I made with Ash. Do you keep forgetting that?" He thinks he's something he's not.

"Yeah, I remember. I don't know how you getting off has anything to do with it. Go educate yourself and then get back to me." I plan to walk away after but then he says the wrong thing.

"Come on, Ash. You got to have fun with the washed-up soccer coach, tell him to leave and find somebody that can actually deal with your bullshit." Once the last word slips from his mouth, I start to walk toward him but what I don't expect is Silas to beat me there and punch his dad in the jaw.

"No, you need to leave. And don't talk about my mom or Jace like that again. He's been there for me this whole time while you were with the fake Barbie. He has been more of a dad than you ever have. You may have fooled mom into thinking that you are so great but you aren't. You're the worst father. I would much rather you have gotten lost while getting milk." I am so proud of this kid. He turns to leave and Layne's hand comes up but I rush over and grab his wrist before he can touch Silas. I twist his arm down and punch him in the eye with my other fist. He's a piece of shit. Nothing else needs to be said. Layne looks between all of us and takes his cue to leave. Smart choice, I would hate to have to kill him. Once the door closes I look at Silas's hand. His knuckles are bloodied.

"Good shot. It's busted, go put some ice on it and I'll wrap it in a minute." I have been in plenty of fights and I have had my fair share of injuries. He leaves and I look at Ash. I'm trying to figure out if I'm in deep shit or if I'm ok. She doesn't give me the chance to ask. She jumps into my arms and laces her fingers through my hair. Tears start falling from her eyes and I kiss them away.

"Thank you. Nobody has ever stood up for me and Silas like that before. I'm sorry that you had to hit him." She tries to get it all out but her sniffling makes it difficult to understand.

"Don't be sorry, I'm sure as hell not. I have been wanting to hit that little bitch for a while. Nobody talks to my family like that. I don't give a shit who it is." I catch her off guard and her eyes widen and more tears fall.

"Your family?" she whimpers.

"My family. I told you, you are it for me. I love Silas like he's mine. I'm too old to be playing around." I lose my breath when she kisses me hard. It's passionate, desperate, intense. I don't want to stop but Silas is waiting for me. I place her on her feet and kiss her forehead. "I'll be right back." Now to find him. My hand is a little sore from that fuckers face. But it was so worth it. I've been wanting to do that every time I saw his face on the sidelines at the games. I turn the corner into the kitchen. He has a stupid ass smile going on.

"What did you do?" It can't be from hitting his dad. I know that smile.

"She's coming over. I texted her and told her that I need help. She's going to take care of me." Kids, fresh eyes, and no broken hearts.

"What's her name?" He has talked about her but never gave a name.

"Cassie Hart," he breathes.

"Ok well, then I'm going to leave you to wait. I'll put condoms in the hallway bathroom. I wouldn't do anything just yet but if it does happen, be safe." I walk away and grab some condoms out of the bedroom.

"What are you doing with those?" Ash walks up behind me. Shit.

"Please don't ask me that." I don't meet her eyes.

"Jace...," she scolds me.

"Silas's girlfriend is coming over but think about this before you freak out, ok. He's going to do it whether you like it or not. Might as well keep him safe." I get all of that out quickly before she reacts.

"I already have condoms where he can get them. I'm not an idiot. You are the only person in this house that is stupid enough to try something without protection." She laughs right there in my face.

"So you have already had the talk with him?" I figured the dumbass father didn't say anything about it. Shit, he probably doesn't know what to tell him. He's clueless.

"Yes, I talked to him about two years ago." Damn that was early. My face must say what I'm thinking. "If you could do the math then you would know that I had Silas when I was fifteen. So yes, I talked to him early in life.

He also knows that I will not be raising a baby that I didn't push out of my vagina. He will have to take on that responsibility. I think I may have scared him a bit with that but whatever works." She is something else.

"Well then, I'm glad you covered most of it." I shouldn't say it but since she wants to be like that to me, I'm going to burst her fucking bubble.

"Most of it?" She sounds confused.

"You didn't tell him to not use a shirt to clean himself up. You can't get clothes back to their softness after that. He should always use tissues or just go do his business in the shower." She looks disgusted with that but it's all true. Before I figured that out, I would go through shirts often. I had to throw the used ones away.

"No part of me wants to talk to him about that. That's what his dad is for," she says and I am instantly annoyed.

"Well, his dad is a fuck up that can't get his shit life together so I'm pretty sure Silas doesn't need to listen to a damn word that guy says." My temper is starting to get the best of me. She takes a step back and holds her hands up in a defensive gesture. I try to take a couple of breaths to calm myself down. "I'm sorry. The guy is a douche and he isn't doing any good with his life. I don't mean to overstep. I just want to be the man that he looks up to." I confess and I feel vulnerable but it comes easy. Her hands are gentle when she puts them on my chest. She gets on her tiptoes and gives me a quick but still sweet kiss.

"That boy just decked his own dad for you. I'm pretty sure he does look up to you. So get yourself together. Go give the kid a condom and tell him to keep himself in his pants. Tell him that she will feel like he's using her if he tries anything right now." That makes me feel better. I don't know why I am in my head so much right now. I don't understand these feelings and now I feel like I'm on a fucking Dr. Phil episode. I get closer to her and lay my head on hers. We stand there for a few minutes and she pushes me away. I smile as I back away from her.

# Chapter 19

## Ash

The week goes by quickly. Work has been busy with people getting iced coffees. It's crazy how hot it got within a week. I'm just glad that tomorrow the weekend starts and I can recover. Well, almost. I still have to take Silas to his game and Coach Jace wants everybody on the field an hour early for warm-ups. I don't like being outside on a spring night. Bugs start to come out and the fucking mosquitoes can suck donkey balls. I can't even voice my opinion during the games anymore. Stupid refs said I would get kicked off the sideline if I kept yelling at them. If they would just do their damn job I wouldn't have to do it for them.

I get tonight to relax and hopefully soothe my thoughts. I walk into my house and all the lights are off except a faint glow from the hallway. I lock my door and pull my knife out of my bag. I'm always prepared to do a little stabby stab when it's needed. I slowly move toward the light. My breathing is getting heavy and I start to sweat. My heart is beating out of my chest. I hold my knife up and turn the corner to my room. I stop and take in what's in front of me. There are a bunch of tea light candles and a couple of actual candles. On my bed is the shape of a heart made out of Reeses. Jace is standing there with a little black jewelry box. My eyes are getting wet and I can't pick my feet up to move. He has on light blue jeans I have always been a fan of and a white shirt with black writing on it.

WILL YOU......

He smirks and slowly steps toward me. My breath catches and I think I'm in shock. Do I need to go to the hospital? Oh God, I can't breathe anymore. He gets down on one knee and my hands cover my mouth.

"Jace... What are you doing?" I didn't realize I was crying. He hasn't looked away since I walked in.

"Ash Miller, I love you so much and I want to spend the rest of my life with you. Make me the happiest man in the world" — He opens the box — "and start building a house with me?" His smile gets big. In the box is a key chain with a red tag on it.

"You are such an asshat! Fuck you, Jace." I start sniffling and laughing at the same time. I am actually relieved that it wasn't a different question because I am not ready for that one. He's still on his knee waiting for an answer. I make a show of myself thinking about it even though building our own house was my idea in the first place.

"I don't know. I mean, you will try to take over and I just can't have that. This is such a big step. I mean, wow." My performance is fun but his smile is starting to drop and he put in so much work for this. I don't want to make him feel shitty. "One condition."

"Yes, you can have a sex room with thick walls. Nobody will hear you scream my name." His smile comes back and I roll my eyes. He thinks he is so funny.

"Actually I wanted to call it my sex dungeon. You know so that I can lock you up and use you whenever I want." His eyes go wide but laughs. There's no way I could actually do that. My confidence is not even close to being that high.

"My leg is actually starting to hurt waiting for your answer." He shifts and I hear a crack. "Don't you dare laugh? I'm fucking old, my body isn't what it was five years ago." He takes a jab at me.

"Yes, I will pretend that you came up with this idea on your own and build a fantastic house with you." I put him out of his misery and he slowly, very slowly actually, stands up. He grunts and groans. Now I know this is just an act. He is so in shape so there's no way it takes him that much effort just to stand up.

"Was taking your sweet time really necessary?" He may be irritated but he's covering it up well.

"I hear that if something is easy then it's not worth it," I say confidently. He wraps his arms around my waist and he stares into my eyes. My body reacts to his strong arms on me. I run my hands up and down his biceps and I bite my bottom lip to keep myself from digging my teeth into him. His ocean-blue eyes darken and I know he feels it too. I think this is the perfect time to show him what I have been working on. My nerves are at an all-time high but I need to do this for him. I want to give him all of me. "So, I want to show you something and since Silas is at his dads', I think it's a good time." I leave his arms and I feel the emptiness as I step away. I get the box from under the bed and open it. His smile widens but he doesn't say anything. "I think I'm ready but please be easy." He walks up to me and takes the box full of lube and butt plugs out of my hands and drops them on the floor. I forgot about the chocolate until he swipes his arm over the bed and they all fall to the floor.

My body starts shaking a little and I almost want to back out but then he starts kissing my palm and up my arm. His lips give me tingles and I press my thighs together. His mouth has been in all of my wet dreams. I let him take the lead this time, mainly because I don't know what I'm doing. He grabs the back of his shirt by the neckline and pulls it over his head to toss it on the floor. The real candles are on top of my dresser so there won't be any fires. Even though I know what his muscles look like, I still look at those abs like it's the first time. He gives me time to take him all in. His jeans sit low on his hips, letting me follow his happy trail down to the beautiful V. I have to stop myself from getting on my knees and licking up the veins that lead to a very hard dick. My time is up when he pulls me to him and lifts me to sit on the foot of the bed.

"I'm going to get a towel because this is going to get messy." He goes to the bathroom and I'm left with my thoughts. Messy? I didn't read anything about it being messy. Oh my God! Am I going to shit all over him? My heart rate picks up and I'm freaking out. He comes back into the room before I can run out. Where would I have even gone? This is my house. He must notice my second thoughts because he stops where he's at.

"We don't have to do this. Really, it's no big deal." He tries to make me feel better.

"What do you mean by messy?" I'm not going to voice what I think he meant.

"All of the lube that I'm going to use. I want to make this as painless as possible for you. What did you think I meant?" There's no way I am answering that.

"Nothing. So, what do we do now?" It's difficult but I'm letting him do whatever it is that he wants to do back there. He leans down and places a gentle kiss on my neck. He toys with the seam at the bottom of my shirt. He slowly pulls it up and over my head. I didn't wear a bra today because, with my tiny boobs, I don't really need one. Apparently, he likes that because he gives me his sexy smirk and his mouth goes straight to my nipples. I have been meaning to change out the jewelry but keep forgetting. Maybe I'll actually remember after this. He licks around my breasts and down to my hip. I lay down to give him better access. I close my eyes and his touch is heightened.

He tugs my waistband down to my ankles and his breath is on my thigh. Chill bumps break out and I shiver. I know he notices how to wound up he has me and he has hardly touched me. My shoes and socks come off with my pants not far behind. He isn't rushing me or just trying to get it in. This is sweet. My legs get cold without his touch so I open my eyes to see what's going on. He's pulling his pants off and he lays the towel out over the head of the bed. The pillows get tossed off and he picks up a bottle of lube and condoms.

I stay where I am and watch him walk to the bedside table and pull out one of my vibrators. He gets the tiny one that's as big as my finger. I'm now confused. I thought he was just going to stick his dick in my ass, why would I need a vibrator? He rolls the condom on himself and walks over to me. He reaches down and picks me up to lay me on the towel. His fingers slide in my wetness and he moves it in little circles. It tickles at first but then I warm up to it and the warmth finds its way from my thighs to my heart. I can't tell if I'm horny or having an emotional breakdown. The familiar heat is building but not enough.

"I'll be right back." He gets up and leaves me lying here with my legs open. The cold hits my wetness and I slam my thighs shut. He walks back in with two shot glasses and a bottle of Jack. *Oh, I like where this is going.* "Just to loosen you up a little. Take the nerves away." He puts the glasses down and fills them to the top. I take one and clink mine with his. I shoot it straight back and the heat runs down my throat. It hits me hard and I cough a couple of times. I'm used to drinking but I always mix it with a coke. I usually never just drink the liquor by itself.

I hear his low laugh he tries to hide but fails. I grab the bottle from him and pour myself another shot. I throw that one back and give it back to him. Two is my limit. I'm a lightweight so anymore and I will be on the floor drunk. He sets everything on the table and walks towards me.

"Are you sure you want to do this? You can say no at any point and I'll stop," he reminds me and it takes me back to when we first got cozy in the bathroom stall.

"It's like deja vu." It takes him a minute to catch on but once he does, his smile hits his eyes. He licks his bottom lip and leans in for a kiss. It starts out sweet but the alcohol is starting to hit me and I deepen it. I jump on him and wrap my legs around his waist. Somehow his dick stayed hard that whole time. I'm not complaining though. He holds my thighs and lays me down on the bed, our lips not breaking away from each other. My tongue pushes for him to open his mouth. He does and I lose all control.

My hands go to his hair and I push his lips on mine even harder, to a point that it should hurt but I'm numb so I can hardly feel anything. I wrap my legs around him tighter and pull his body against me even more. His teeth find my lip and pulls. Fuck. I love this man. He knows exactly what I want. He lets go and pulls my hair back, exposing my neck. I thought he was going to kiss it like he usually does but this time he bites down. My mouth opens wide and I let out an embarrassing sound. He bites his way down to my breast and sucks on one nipple while his other hand lets go of my hair and squeezes the other. I grind my hips on him, needing some type of release. He moves on to biting the dip in my side. I am going crazy.

"Fuck me already," I try to say but my words are breathy.

"What's the word," he prompts and I can't think straight. I don't know what the fuck he's talking about. "The word, Ash. How will I know to stop?" Oh right.

"Pineapple," I let the word fall from my lips and he's pleased enough that he gets up and turns me over to my knees. He picks the lube up and squeezes the bottle all over my ass. It's cold and sticky. His hands are on me the next second and he's wiping it down to the hole that I never thought to shove something into. I feel more of the cold liquid getting rubbed around my hole. He coats his pinky in it and then slowly starts to push it into me. There's a sharp pain at first but then he keeps his hand still. It feels like his whole finger is in there.

"Shh, relax. It will stop hurting if you think about something else and slow your breathing down," he soothes in a deep timber like it's the easiest thing to do.

"How can I relax when you have your whole finger in there?" I whisper so that he doesn't hear how bad this is for me.

"It's the tip of my smallest finger. I wouldn't do that to you. Do you trust me?" *ONLY THE TIP?? There's no way!* I try to calm myself down. It takes a minute or two but when my heart stops pounding out of my chest, I answer him.

"Yes. You can keep going." He pulls his finger out and pours more lube on it. Then he goes back to where he was. This time it slides in with no problem.

"I'm going to go in a little deeper. Just keep your breathing slow." He pours more and more lube on his finger with each push. He takes his time with it and eventually he is all the way in. He starts to wiggle his pinky around to stretch me out.

"Are you ready for me now?" he asks and I'm nervous but I told him that I would do this so I'm going to see it through.

"Let's do it." I don't have to look back to know he's smiling.

"Get the vibrator that's beside you and make yourself cum," he orders while he is covering the condom with so much lube that I could swim in it. I see the mess that he was talking about. I do as he says and turn my vibrator on. I feel his head slowly pushing into me. I push my little friend on my clit and my other arm gives out. My face is now kissing the bed and my ass is straight up. I'm trying to concentrate on the vibrations but the pinching feeling in my ass is a little bit more powerful. He stops with every inch that goes in and pours more lube on him. He's going to go through the whole damn bottle before we even finish.

"Are you ok?" he moans.

"Yes, I'm good," I say honestly. I thought it was going to be a lot worse than this.

"I'm going to need you to cum," his voice is low and rough. I bring my mind back to the good feeling building between my legs. It doesn't take long before I'm cumming and I don't stop. I feel like I'm never going to stop. Just when I think the feeling is slowing down, I feel his hips on me. He pulls almost all the way out and then slams into me and I shout. I don't do it because it hurts, it actually feels good and I keep cumming. He's actually fucking my ass now and it feels weird but still really good. His hand comes down and slaps my ass.

"Oh fuck! Yes, yes, yes. Keep doing that." I drop the vibrator and lift myself back on my hands. I toss my hair over my shoulder so that I can look back at him. His jaw is clenched and his eyes are on me. "You make me feel so good. Keep fucking me like this. We are doing this every time." I moan loudly.

"Damn, I love you. All of you," he confesses and I'm cumming again but this time he comes with me. When we both finish he leans down and kisses my back. I start laughing because I can't believe we just did that and I liked it. He pulls out and it feels so weird. He goes straight to the bathroom and a couple of minutes later I hear the bath running.

"Come on, let's ease the soreness." He comes and picks me up bridal style. When we get to the bathroom I tell him I can stand on my own and he puts me down.

"Thank you for doing that with me." I didn't expect him to say that but he always makes me feel like I'm special.

The soccer game just finished and the boys are all jumping up and down in excitement. They just won their last game. Silas told me before the game started they were going to one of the boy's houses and staying the night there. Layne was fine with it since it was his weekend and he wouldn't have to spend time with him. I can't believe I thought he was a good dad.

"START STRONG, FINISH STRONG!" They all yell and then Jace makes them take a knee for his speech. I get a text from Clara so I step away. I get distracted easily and I don't want her to think that I'm ignoring her when I forget to respond.

**CLARA: So, is it over??**

**ME: Yes it is.**

**CLARA: Really? You are going to keep me in suspense!!**

**ME: They won, duh!!!**

> **CLARA: Next weekend I'm going to buy him a cake! I'm so happy for him!**

> **ME: I will let him know you said congrats.**

The kids are all running to a navy van where the mom of one of the boys is standing. I turn and see Jace watching me.

"Don't be a creep!" I yell out to him. He just smiles and shakes his head. The van drives off and Jace passes by me and goes to his car. Izzy pulls up beside him on her motorcycle. She wasn't joking, she actually has one. I have got to talk her into letting me ride on the back one day. Jace gets in his and cranks it up. I look at him confused. Is he leaving without saying anything? The music starts blasting out of his still-opened door. *Slow Dance In A Parking Lot* by Jordan Davis comes on. At least he has good taste in music. He turns his headlights on and he walks towards me.

"Will you dance with me?" he asks me while he pulls me to the field. I wrap my arms around his neck and his hands hold my waist. We start to sway from side to side.

"This is the most cheesy thing you have ever done." I smile up at him.

"Maybe, but you like it." He kisses me slowly and passionately.

"I love you." I try not to let my eyes water up.

"I love you too. Can we start planning out our house now?" That makes a tear fall and I am so happy. This man was well worth the wait and I can't believe I get to spend forever with him.

# Epilogue–Ash

ONE YEAR LATER

"Y'all built a beautiful home, Ash," Izzy says after we walk her through the house. It's finally done and we are all moved in. Since Jace doesn't cook, I didn't have to throw out any of his kitchen gadgets, I wasn't going to part with mine. Actually, I made him get rid of all of his furniture. Everything that was there was bought to start a life with his ex. Fuck that. It might have been petty but it is what it is. I'm not going to have some other bitches stuff in my – our – house.

"Thank you, it took a lot of arguing," I tell her and it's the truth. It was not an easy ride.

"Ok, so we aren't talking about all of the hitting you did?" Jace jokes. He thinks he's funny.

"If you weren't such an asshat then it wouldn't have happened," I deadpan.

"Well, it was your smartass that started it." Jace snaps back. I keep to myself so that we don't get back to the craziness.

"Ok, well then. I brought y'all a housewarming gift." Izzy runs out to her car and Jace and I stand there in silence. When she comes back she's holding a frame that is almost as big as her.

"Damn, Izzy. You didn't have to get us anything," I inform her as Jace helps her turn it around so that I can see. It's a framed picture of me and Jace on the soccer field.

"It's beautiful, Izzy. Thank you," Jace announces.

"Wait, is that from last year when Jace pulled me out to dance? Is that why you were there that night? I completely forgot about you driving up that night." It all clicks together.

"I was actually trying to watch the game but some people had me tied up." Izzy stares off into space. "I miss those girls. I wonder what they are up to now." She thinks out loud.

"Thank you, I love it," I squeal as I give her a hug.

"Jace told me how you have a love for pictures and I saw the opportunity. It took a lot for me to keep this quiet for so fucking long. I wanted to wait for dumb-dumb to propose but it hasn't happened yet and I'm tired of keeping it a secret." Izzy rolls her eyes at Jace.

"I have plans, don't you worry," Jace remarks. Secretly I have been waiting too but I'm not going to push it. I have my man and our house and of course, my son whom Jace calls his. I can't be any happier.

# Acknowledgments

I would like to thank all of you for giving me a chance and reading Taking The Shot. At first, I didn't think that I could do it but once I started typing, it flowed easily.

Ok, so here is my award-winning speech. AHH! Sorry, that was my internal screaming. I just can't believe I made it here. Anyways, moving on to what y'all are actually back here for.

Ashley and Bethany, y'all have been so supportive and helping every step of the way. Thank y'all for putting my book (and me) before everything else. Y'all have been my rock through this whole thing. I fully expect you both to deal with me and my attitude forever. Yes, you both are here forever.

Also, Carmen Carmen Carmen.... Girl, you have made miracles happen. Thank you for the cover, logo, and my millions of questions! Thank you for helping me get through this and showing me how to pull it all together. You are the best and God has put you in my life for a reason. You are amazing.

Thank you Kate (Katie) for all of the late-night sprints. I don't think I could have written as much as I did without you. Also, the way you helped me set this baby up, I could never repay you.

I want to thank my three kids for their support. Obviously they have no idea what this book is about but they still pushed me every day. My daughter constantly asked if I met my word count goal for the day and she did not cut me any slack. My oldest son gave me advice on the soccer games and my youngest son helped me remember that sometimes you just need to step away from the computer and take a nap together on the couch.

Thank you Cara for letting me have down time at your house and supplying wine while I write. You're the best.

I would say lastly but I know that I'm missing people and I am so sorry.

Thank you, Alyssa, the best sister-in-law. Talking to you and my perfect niece and nephew every day has kept me going.

# About Author

S.L.Forrester is the author of Spice, Sass, and HEAs'. She lives in South Carolina with her husband and 3 kids. When she isn't writing, she's either dancing in her living room or reading. She listens to anything from country to 90s music and she reads fantasy and smut. Loads of smut. She cares for her friends like they are family.

If you want to follow her for future writings, look her up on Instagram and Tiktok.

@S.L.Forrester

www.ingramcontent.com/pod-product-compliance
Lightning Source LLC
LaVergne TN
LVHW010312070526
838199LV00065B/5533